LIKE A LAIRD TO A FLAME

Irvines of Drum
Book Two

Mia Pride

ARE YOU SIGNED UP FOR DRAGONBLADE'S BLOG?

You'll get the latest news and information on exclusive giveaways, exclusive excerpts, coming releases, sales, free books, cover reveals and more.

Check out our complete list of authors, too!

No spam, no junk. That's a promise!

Sign Up Here

www.dragonbladepublishing.com

Dearest Reader;

Thank you for your support of a small press. At Dragonblade Publishing, we strive to bring you the highest quality Historical Romance from the some of the best authors in the business. Without your support, there is no 'us', so we sincerely hope you adore these stories and find some new favorite authors along the way.

Happy Reading!

CEO, Dragonblade Publishing

Additional Dragonblade books by Author Mia Pride

Irvines of Drum Series
For Love of a Laird (Book 1)
Like a Laird to a Flame (Book 2)
Maid for the Knight (Book 3)

*** Please visit Dragonblade's website for a full list of books and authors. Sign up for Dragonblade's blog for sneak peeks, interviews, and more: ***
www.dragonbladepublishing.com

Dedication

To all of my kin in the Irvine Clan and all of those
who came before us.

Our history is rich and our legacy continues.

CHAPTER ONE

December – 1411
Dunnottar Castle, Scotland

T EMPLES THROBBING, HE closed his eyes and slowly nodded, no
longer knowing what he was even nodding about. No treaty was
worth this torture. His clan laughed in the hall of Dunnottar Castle
while enjoying a meal, but all William Keith could hear was the
incessant blathering of the child beside him, brought to him as a
prospective bride.

Nothing the lass said had made any sense since the moment she
began talking about her maid plaiting her hair too tightly, causing her
a headache. If only he could explain that her very existence was
causing him one, as well. He was the laird of the Keiths and Marischal
of Scotland, the king's own protector, by the devil! Must he truly suffer
these constant visits by neighboring clans, forcing what he could only
believe to be the most unsavory choices for wives on to him?

"My papa says ye just arrived home from Drum Castle, aye?" Marjorie Douglas, the creature bordering on woman and child beside him,
asked.

Opening his eyes and doing his best to focus on her through the
bewilderment clouding his vision, William nodded and took a rather

large bite from the hunk of boar's meat still resting on his trencher, doing his best to avoid eye contact with the red-haired bane of his existence. "Aye. My sister just married their laird, Robert Irvine, four months past. I visit frequently now that we have finally achieved peace between our clans."

Marjorie sighed and scooted her chair closer to his, resting her elbows on the table. "Have ye met Reginald Irvine, the laird's brother?"

William scoffed and almost spit his mouthful of food out. Aye, he had met Reginald. They were friendly now, but it had only been a few months ago when Reginald participated in an outrageous scheme pretending to have married Elizabeth, William's sister. It had turned out to be a ploy to make Robert jealous enough to prove he loved her, and it had worked. William could not entirely begrudge the man, yet his name always made William reflexively scowl. "Aye, I ken the man."

"Ye do?" Marjorie seemed much too interested, and William dared to look at the lass. Eyes alight, she leaned in closer, her freckles only making her look even more like a child than her twin plaited red hair did.

"My laird! A missive has arrived for ye from Drum Castle!" The sconces along the walls of his keep flickered as the winter's cold invaded the room, flakes of snow drifting in just as the doors slammed shut. His messenger, Aldrich, stepped forward looking windswept, his dark blond hair tangled around his head, patches of red gracing his cheeks and nose. Yet, the lassies all stared at him in awe, and William shook his head and sighed. Aldrich had always had that effect on the women of Dunnottar Castle. Thankfully, Marjorie seemed enamored, as well, and William was glad of the distraction.

"Many thanks, Aldrich," William replied, putting a hand out to retrieve the missive. "Please rest. It is mighty frigid outside. The snow has yet to cease all day."

"Aye, my laird. 'Tis frightful, yet nothing I am unaccustomed to." A few women tittered and whispered in one another's ear, most likely about finding ways to warm his flesh. William simply smiled and pointed toward the fire raging in his large hearth. "Be that as it may, we have a fire and plenty of food. Please make yerself comfortable and enjoy the feast."

"Thank ye, my laird." Aldrich bowed and walked toward the hearth and William noticed how young Marjorie's eyes followed his every step. The lass was fortunately interested in many different men, which pleased him greatly. The true concern would be finding a way to inform her father, the mighty laird of the Douglas Clan.

As the eldest living son of the man known as the Black Douglas, Archibald was no less dark than the former earl. Though that title had come to refer to their entire line, this man had more than earned the title, and rumor had it that his sons were just as devious. And while no marriage sounded appealing to William, he was nearly thirty years of age and had avoided the task long enough. With conflict around every corner, he needed allies, strong ones. None were stronger than the Douglases whose lands spread across Scotland and influence spread across Europe. With Archibald being married to the sister of King Robert, the previous monarch of Scotland, their power was boundless and they were known to be a mighty ally. But, they would also make a mighty foe and while William was certain he did not wish for this match with Marjorie, he was not at all certain how to address his issue without causing insult.

"Well, what does it say?" Marjorie asked, leaning somehow even closer. William clenched his teeth and closed his eyes before he was caught rolling them. The chit was wearing on his last nerve. Breaking the wax seal of the Laird of Drum, his brother-by-marriage, William unfolded the parchment and began to read the missive, dreading bad news. He trusted his sister, Elizabeth, in the hands of Robert, who truly loved her dearly, but he was away often on business and William

3

always worried about his wee sister.

His anxiety washed away as he finished reading and folded it up once more. "'Tis an invitation to join them for the Yule this year," he said slowly, wondering if this was just his chance to break away from Marjorie and her father. Yet, he was meant to host them for the Yule at Dunnottar and leaving for Drum, no matter how tempting, would be an insult as grand as rejecting Archibald's distressing daughter.

"Och!" Marjorie clapped her hands together once and smile widely. "Are ye going to go?"

Shaking his head, William leaned over and looked at her father, who sat in the seat next to her, remaining eerily quiet most meals. After several failed attempts, William had decided over the last few days that mayhap Archibald simply preferred silence. No wonder he was desperate to pawn his daughter off on an unfortunate man, for she had no concept of silence or decorum in the slightest.

"Nay. I cannae. I am to host the Yule here. Though Elizabeth does say she wouldnae have asked, only there is a pressing matter she wishes to discuss with me." William tapped his finger on the rough wooden surface of the head table, pushing his reddish-blond hair away from his face as he thought. What matter could be so pressing that Elizabeth would dare to ask him away from his own people and duties during the Yuletide?

"I would love to meet yer sister, William, and some of the other members of the Irvine Clan..." William shifted his knowing gaze between Marjorie and Archibald, an idea forming in his mind that was mildly cruel, and yet delightfully canny. The lass was clearly smitten with Reginald Irvine, and after the ruse he had pulled during the summer, making everyone believe he had married Elizabeth in secret and almost destroying peace between the clans, William decided Reg owed him a mighty favor.

"I do believe ye would enjoy their company verra much, Marjorie. 'Tis a pity I shall have to write to Lizzie and explain that I cannae attend. After all, I am pleased to host ye and members of yer clan for the Yule here at Dunnottar."

"That willnae be necessary." For the first time all meal, Archibald spoke. "I received a missive from the Lady of Drum, inviting Marjorie and me to join their clan for the Yule, along with the Douglas kin in attendance here. And I intend to accept." Marjorie squealed like a mouse having his tail stepped on by a large booted man and rapidly clapped her hands.

William pursed his lips and sat straight up in his seat. The man was intentionally insulting him, insinuating he would rather spend the Yule elsewhere, yet William knew what was truly occurring. It was quite clear William had no interest in Marjorie and from what he had heard throughout the Lowlands, he was not the first prospective groom to be dissuaded by her favors, or lack thereof. Archibald would stack suiter upon suiter until he found a man who needed an alliance with the Douglases more than he needed to keep his sanity for the remainder of his days. And though the Douglas Clan would indeed be a strong ally for the Keiths, William was not that man.

"I am pleased to hear that, Archie." He truly was. He would enjoy spending time with Robert and Elizabeth while watching Reginald squirm in discomfort. Finally having peace with the Irvines after generations of wars and unrest between their clans was truly a blessing and one he gave Elizabeth all the credit for. Nothing had been easy for her since the papers were drafted for the treaty when she was a wee lass. One man after another passed away and she felt pawned off until she finally fell in love with Robert, with help from the schemes of Reginald. Though William now was fond of the man, he still would enjoy torturing him a wee bit.

Suddenly, a conversation he remembered hearing once at Drum resurfaced and William leaned across Marjorie, surprised she had remained silent for longer than a minute. "I ken ye are not fond of the Irvines. Do ye not have some old rivalry?"

"Aye. The Douglas Clan doesnae mix with the likes of the Irvines." Archibald turned toward William, his graying hair and dark eyes catching his attention. The man's features gave nothing away. Pushing away from the table, Archie stood at his full massive height and stretched, groaning loud enough to make even the noisiest voices in the room stop mid-word to stare at the man. "But how shall progress ever be achieved if we hold on to old grudges, aye?"

Squinting his eyes, William looked at the man, still unable to read his true intentions. Did he really hope for peace with the Irvines and potentially a marriage agreement, or did he hope to gain access to Drum only to cause trouble? William would not trust the man, yet he had been here for several days without issue and whether William liked it or not, Elizabeth already invited the Douglas Clan to attend the Yule.

Deciding he would simply have to keep a close eye on Archibald while at Drum, William smiled and rose from his seat, more than ready to be done with this exhausting meal and away from this exacerbating lass. "Aye. I cannae agree more. I will inform my dear sister to expect us all for the Yule and prepare for my people, who will be just fine without me here, I am certain."

With the Yule beginning in just a few days, William could not help but wonder why Elizabeth gave such short notice, nor what was so pressing, Still, he was surprised by how much he anticipated his journey back to Drum. Never did he believe he would be excited to break bread with the Irvine brothers, and none of that even had to do with his interest in pushing Marjorie Douglas onto Reginald Irvine. He knew the man would not accept the lass, but William smiled to himself as he left the table and headed for the stairs leading up to the tower as he imagined the look on the man's face when he met her for the first time.

"DO BE CAREFUL, Mary. Ye are starting to consume more food than the swine in the pen."

"Reg!" Elizabeth exclaimed with a gasp. "Have ye no shame? She is carrying yer brother's child!"

"Ye ken he doesnae," Mary replied, throwing a bit of bread across the table, successfully connecting with Reginald's left eye before landing near his hand. "Besides. I would rather eat like a swine than look like one."

"Oh-ho!" Reginald said with a chuckle and popped the piece of bread into his mouth. "Consider me successfully insulted. If Alex were still alive, he would be most proud of yer barbs."

Mary looked at Elizabeth, wondering if she would cringe at the sound of Alexander's name, yet all she did was smile fondly, and Mary did the same. Aye, she was seven months along in her pregnancy with Alex's child, but he had been Elizabeth's husband for a short time before falling in battle. Mary touched Elizabeth's shoulder and thought about how odd life was. She and Alex had been in love when he had been forced to wed with Elizabeth Keith to solidify peace between their clans. Nothing had ever pained Mary more than losing Alex to Elizabeth, except for the news of his death. And yet, somehow, the two women had become great companions during their trials. Elizabeth had never truly loved Alex and, in the end, she remarried his younger brother, Robert and had found true love.

As for Mary, well, she would never love another man for the rest of her days. She was large with child and rather pleased to live without a husband, yet everyone insisted she must marry. Not a single man in the Irvine Clan could ever take Alexander's place and marrying one of his kin felt like a betrayal to his memory. Nay, she had loved once, more than some ever love in a lifetime, and she would raise her child alone and cherish the memories and know that she once had what others only dreamed of.

"If Alex was still alive, he would box yer ears for comparing his woman to a swine," Robert added wryly, coming behind Elizabeth and wrapping his arms around her before kissing the top of her head. Mary smiled and felt a mixture of happiness and pain. She loved to see Elizabeth and Robert so happy and in love, yet the ache she still felt every time she thought of Alex, every time she remembered the feel of him embracing her, still knocked the wind from her lungs. He would not be here to witness their child being born. Rubbing her swollen belly, Mary stood up from her seat and forced a shaky smile, praying nobody felt her weakness.

"Aye, he would. Although he quite enjoyed any excuse to knock Reginald on his arse. As for me, I grow weary and require sleep. This child grows heavier by the moment, I vow." Looking at Elizabeth, she saw her friend's smile falter and knew that her sadness was apparent. But naught could be done and none could blame her. She had once had love, companionship, and the chance at happiness with a man. Now, her child would give her those things, and she was glad of it. No man could possibly replace Alex and, though she knew her friends wished for her to find a man, Mary was grateful that none had been forced upon her. As laird and the uncle to her child, Robert had the power and the motive to see her settled.

"Ye ken I always let him win, Mary!" Reginald hollered after her as she started toward the stairs leading up to her tower chamber. Laughing loudly, she did not bother to turn around or respond, for all knew well enough that Alexander had been the strongest of the three brothers, though just barely. The hall was festively decorated for the Yule with mistletoe hanging from the rafters and evergreens hanging from the screens or draped across the stair railings. This was Mary's favorite time of year and with each day, new guests arrived to share in the joy and celebration. Yet, for Mary, any joy she felt would be short-lived. A small laugh here, a forced smile there. Nay, no true happiness could be had during the Yuletide without Alex's blue eyes to gaze into, his wit to contend with, or his strong arms to keep her warm.

An ache had settled into her bones as of late and the winter's chill did her no favors, though she should not complain. Louisa had birthed her son in the middle of the summer and though Scotland was no desert, the swelling of her limbs from being overheated was not something Mary envied. Back aching and feet throbbing, Mary grunted as she made it up to the third floor of the tower, feeling decades older than her twenty years.

Reaching her chamber, Mary sighed as she opened the door and kicked off her leather slippers just as the bairn kicked and she let out a small yelp.

"Wean kicking ye in the ribs, once more, aye?"

Yelping once more, but this time with fear, Mary placed her hand on her wildly beating heart and let out a deep breath when she saw Elizabeth's maid, Matilda, tending to the fire in the hearth near the corner.

"Goodness, Tilda! Ye will make my pains come on too early if ye scare me like that!"

Brushing her red coiled locks away with the inside of her wrist to avoid getting soot on her face, Matilda smiled apologetically and stepped forward. "Och, I apologize, Mary. I only wished to see to it that ye and the bairn would be warm for the night."

Matilda was only two years younger than Mary, yet somehow she seemed so much younger with her slim waist and unburdened body. Mary would never take the ability to simply walk without feeling like a boulder was between her legs for granted ever again. "Thank ye, Tilda, but ye ken ye dinnae need to do such things for me. I am naught but a maid, myself, now that Elizabeth is the lady of the castle."

Waving her away, Matilda turned back to the fire and poked at it for a moment, making the flames leap higher as they devoured the wood and moss used as fodder. "Nonsense. Aside from carrying the former laird's child and the current laird's nephew or niece," she said with a wink, clearly hoping for a wee lassie, "ye are a woman carrying a child and deserve comfort, Mary, no matter yer station. I do hope if I ever am unfortunate enough to take a husband and have a child, that ye would do the same for me."

That made Mary laugh. True genuine laughter was hard to come by, but Matilda always knew just what to say. "Of course, I would. Thank ye." The bairn kicked her in the ribs once more, and she cringed. Yet another thing she would never take for granted: not having a wee human wedged beneath her bones.

"Come, Mary." Walking over to the bed, Matilda pulled the covers back and patted the soft mattress. "Ye need to get some rest. Tomorrow will be a busy day. Many guests are on their way and should arrive by the evening meal."

"Oh?" Feeling lulled to sleep by both the warmth radiating from the hearth and the thought of curling up into her sheets, praying not to have any more of those awful leg cramps during the night, Mary yawned and stretched. "Who will be joining the clan for the Yule this year? Shall the Macleans travel all the way from the Highlands to be here?"

Matilda hastily loosened the ties on Mary's bodice and she breathed deeply, glad to feel her heavy linen gown slide to the floor. Her under tunic was as light as air and she slid into bed, enjoying the cool covers against her legs. Curse her sore, enlarged breasts for aching all day long, and somehow even more so once out of the confines of her bodice.

"Nay, but Elizabeth mentioned that the Douglases would be joining us. Tensions have been high and they were visiting at Dunnottar with her brother, William. She decided to extend them an invitation with intentions to make an alliance and, most unfortunately, they accepted." Matilda scowled and rolled her eyes.

Flashbacks of William's previous visit made Mary crinkle her nose. What was it about Elizabeth's brother that made her want to kick him in the shin every time she saw him? Aye, he was kind enough and clearly cared for his sister, but when he had first arrived at Drum Castle, he had been overly pompous and controlling, often filled with too many complaints about the Irvine brothers, who obviously mattered a great deal to her, as she carried the eldest's unborn child. Mayhap a part of her resented him for marrying his sister to Alexander in the first place, yet she knew that was nobody's fault. Still, having a person to blame gave her a place to direct her ire and William had always made a good target.

"Well then. The Douglases shall be in attendance. That is a good thing, aye? I dinnae ken why ye frown, Tilda."

"They are a sordid lot, Mary, ye ken. They are the Black Douglases and I dinnae trust them. Besides, they are arriving here with Marjorie, the laird's daughter. She is simply atrocious and crazed for all the lads. Though she has never been to Drum, she was at a festival we attended on Fraser lands and couldnae stop following Reg. Verily, she fancies herself in love with the man." Matilda made a gagging gesture and, not for the first time, Mary wondered if Matilda had feelings for Reginald that she cared to keep silent. Though he was above her station as the laird's brother and a noble-born man, he and Matilda seemed to mix well and be the cause of too much mischief on most days, including the plot a few months ago to fake a marriage between him and Elizabeth simply to make Robert jealous and realize how much he cared for her.

"Thankfully, she was visiting Dunnottar to explore a potential marriage between her and William. Hopefully, she will be besotted enough with him by now to leave Reg alone," Matilda added, and Mary frowned.

"William is spending the Yule here, as well?"

"Aye. He is Elizabeth's brother, after all, and he was hosting the Douglas Clan. Lizzie wouldnae invite her brother without inviting his guests... between me and ye, 'tis the only reason she invited them along in the first place. I dinnae think she wants William to match with Marjorie and be saddled with her for a lifetime. I sense she wished a better match for him and already kens who she prefers."

Pulling the covers over herself, Mary crinkled her brow, curiosity driving her to ask more questions. It seemed she was always on the outside of the gossip these days.

"Who does she wish William to wed?"

Shrugging, Matilda snuffed out a candle resting on the table beside the bed and waved away the smoke. "I dinnae ken. She never said and I never asked. But any lass is better than Marjorie Douglas, of that, we can all agree. I only hope she leaves Reg alone while she is here."

Mary pursed her lips to hide a smile. Matilda seemed to care an awful lot about who Reginald wed. "Well then, I suppose we have a lot to prepare for on the morrow," Mary added with a stretch and a yawn.

"Ye have naught to prepare for but birthing this child! Ye willnae lift a cursed finger, ye ken?"

"I am not helpless, Tilda. I am with child! And dinnae forget I was running this keep well before ye and Elizabeth arrived." Indignance was Mary's most frequent emotion as of late. It seemed nobody felt she was good for anything other than breeding, but she was not a broodmare, curse it all. She was an Irvine lass and would do all she could to be involved and keep distracted from the unpleasantness that was William Keith, Laird of Dunnottar and Marischal of Scotland, for his very presence made her wish to pull the hair on his arm just to make him yelp. Just one hair... that's all it would require. She smiled wickedly at that thought and caught Matilda eyeing her oddly.

"As ye say. We shall see what needs doing in the morn. Sleep well, Mary." The sincerity in Matilda's voice helped to placate Mary, and she wished her companion a good night before rolling over in her bed, hoping to dream of being in Alexander's arms, and determined to avoid William Keith at all cost once he arrived.

CHAPTER TWO

WHEN THE FAMILIAR tower of Drum Castle finally showed in the snowy distance, William sighed and looked up at the gray wall of clouds overhead. Usually, he enjoyed traveling in the winter months very much. The snow was never a deterrent for him, nor was the wind. No force on this earth could be a greater burden during his travels than the one riding beside him on a white horse, complaining of the elements as if she had never seen a flake of snow in her entire six and ten years of life.

"Is it colder than usual? It feels colder than usual," Marjorie said for the third time in the past hour, and William sighed inwardly, tightly gripping the reins of his horse with his gloved hands, cherishing every stride that brought him closer to Drum.

"Our destination is just there, on the horizon. We shall arrive shortly, Marjorie." Somehow, he found the will to remain calm and kept a soothing tone, a hard feat for a man known for his quick ire.

"Marjorie! Haud yer wheesht, lass! Ye willnae ever find a husband if all ye do is run yer mouth, ye cursed fool."

Receiving a firm scolding from her father, Marjorie frowned but did as she was commanded and very dramatically pursed her lips together to make a show of obedience, but William would bet his best horse that the lass would be complaining once more before they arrived.

The winter solstice was tomorrow, which meant the Yule would officially begin, and he looked forward to twelve days of merriment and wassailing with his family from both the Keith and Irvine Clans. Between the Keiths and the Douglases, William had over fifty men arriving with him, and one very unpleasant lass.

"Are we almost there? 'Tis awful cold." William breathed out a frustrated breath, seeing wisps escape from his mouth and curl into the cold air. It felt like it was his very soul being sucked out of his body by this Douglas succubus, but he simply shook his head and looked straight ahead.

"William?"

"Aye?" he replied curtly.

"What is Reginald like?"

"Ye have met him, aye?"

"Aye..." she said slowly from beside him but he vowed not to make eye contact. "He was quite occupied when we met. He wished to spend more time with me, I ken, but he was continually pulled away by some insufferable maid who dinnae seem to ken her place."

"Ye speak of Matilda, Elizabeth's maid. And aye, she kens her place well. She is beloved by the Irvines and though she behaves boldly for a servant, she is family to Elizabeth and a companion to Reginald. Ye would do yerself a favor to remember that and respect her if ye wish to earn the respect of the Irvines. If ye wish to meet Reginald upon our arrival, I shall make it so."

"Ye will?" Her voice squeaked, and he smiled like a cat about to trap a mouse.

"With pleasure."

Fortunately, his promise put her in better spirits, and the rest of the journey continued with moderate silence with the sounds of wind and the crunching of fresh snow beneath the hooves of horses to occupy him. White flakes fell on his plaid, a stark contrast against the dark green and blue of Keith colors he wore proudly. It was a satisfying feeling to arrive on Irvine lands and know himself as an ally rather than an enemy in danger. Too many had died in the rivalry over the years, even innocent children that his clan had shamefully set afire without his father's knowledge. It had started a most dark time between the neighboring clans and had escalated the feud from simple cattle raids to all-out war anytime a Keith crossed paths with an Irvine.

Now, thanks to Elizabeth, the clans were at peace. Mayhap she was with child and that was the news she was so eager to share. A child born of their union would work to solidify the peace for all time and a male heir would mean the next Laird of Drum would share Keith blood.

Just as darkness began to set in and the gentle snow threatened to become an aggressive storm, his entourage arrived at the gates of Drum, being immediately signaled to enter by the guards who obviously expected their party.

"Yuletide greetings, Marischal," Anthony, one of their best guards and warriors shouted as his men opened the gates. Our laird and lady have expected ye."

"Many thanks, Anthony!" he shouted back and whistled to his men, urging them to follow him into the outer bailey where the stables and the chapel, where Elizabeth had first married Alexander, and then Robert, were located. The tall, dark, stone walls of Drum towered overhead, surrounded by forest land on most sides, unlike Dunnottar which was nestled on a cliff overlooking the sea. At night, William heard waves crashing against the cliffsides while he slept, herring gulls calling out as they flew around the shore. Here at Drum, the sounds of leaves rustling in the wind while wild animals made themselves known had consumed the night instead. However, with winter upon them, he doubted many leaves or animals were still to be found in the Royal Forest of Drum.

Once William saw Finlay, the elderly stable master, standing by with his stable workers to see to the many newly arrived horses, he dismounted and greeted the old man who he remembered Elizabeth was quite fond of.

"Welcome back to Drum Castle, Marischal," Finlay said with a respectful bow. "We have room in our stables for all the horses though it shall be a tight fit."

"I trust ye to take care of them, Finlay. My sister grew up on horses and loves the creatures dearly. She speaks highly of ye, so I ken ye truly are a master of yer craft."

Beaming, the old man smiled, pulling his Irvine plaid closer to his chest as the storm winds howled and blew wildly. "Thank ye, Marischal."

Nodding, William turned to help Marjorie off her horse, dismayed when she clung on a wee bit too tight and most definitely too long. He had hoped she had diverted her interests elsewhere, yet as he placed her down, she verily dug her claws into his back.

When the doors of Drum's keep flew open, William smiled and forgot all about Marjorie as his sister ran out into the cold, arms wide open to greet him. "Will! Och! 'Tis good to have ye back at Drum for the Yule!"

"I am glad to be back," he said, meaning it with all his heart. He had meant to spend the Yule at Dunnottar, but Drum felt like his second home, and Elizabeth beamed with obvious contentment. William truly owed Robert for treating his sister so well.

Robert stepped up beside Elizabeth and put out his arm. "Greetings, William. Welcome back to Drum." Robert was a tall, muscular man with dark hair and blue eyes, much different than William who had reddish-blond hair and light green, almost yellow, eyes, much like his sister. Yet they were built rather similarly, both having been trained to fight at a young age and serving as warriors in more wars than he cared to consider.

"Thank ye for inviting me to join ye. 'Tis a pleasure to be back." William shook Robert's outstretched forearm and began to speak when he was interrupted by the sound of Marjorie clearing her throat beside him.

"Are ye going to introduce me, Will?" she asked sweetly, making a show of gripping his arm just as he saw Reginald, Matilda, and the woman he remembered as Alexander's mistress appear at the entrance. Her name escaped him, but he recalled that she was with child and by the look of her, she was ready to give birth any day. They had interacted on more than one occasion, but between the Battle of Harlaw calling them away, Alexander's death, and the ridiculous situation with Elizabeth deciding which Irvine brother to marry, the red-haired lass' name escaped him, though her temper did not. She had been rather headstrong and free with her opinions if he recalled.

Looking from Marjorie to his sister and Robert, he saw her smirk and knew Elizabeth was amused by the show, awaiting his introduction.

"Robert and Elizabeth, as ye ken, I have arrived with the Douglas Clan, who was staying with us at Dunnottar. Please meet Archibald, the Earl of Douglas, and his daughter, Miss Marjorie of Douglas."

"I am pleased to meet ye and welcome ye both to Drum," Robert said to Archibald, putting his arm out in greeting. "I am Robert Irvine, Laird of Drum, and this is my wife, Lady Elizabeth."

"Aye, I ken who ye are," Archibald replied, not bothering to clasp forearms with Robert. "We grow weary and my men crave ale. I presume ye Irvines have ale?"

Elizabeth looked at Robert and frowned before looking at William. He could see she was flustered by the earl's cold demeanor, but he wasn't called the Black Douglas for nothing. He was said to have a heart of stone and blood so cold that not even the snow in the dead of winter could compare. William shook his head at Elizabeth and she cleared her throat, looking at Archibald with a forced smile.

"Aye, of course, we do. The finest ale and mead to be sure."

"I am tired and cold, Will," Marjorie said loudly, making sure all eyes suddenly focused on her petulant facial expression. Huddling closer to his side, Marjorie looked behind Robert and Elizabeth in search of Reginald and as soon as she spotted him, a smile spread across her thin lips.

"Why do ye not all follow us into the keep? Tomorrow we shall light the Yule log and serve mince pies but, for today, we have a fire in the hearth and a boar roasting for all to enjoy," Elizabeth said.

"And much ale," Robert replied flatly before turning on his heels, taking Elizabeth's arm and leading the way to the hall.

This was not going well, not that he expected it to. Whatever reason Elizabeth had to invite him here must be of great importance if she invited the Black Douglas just to ensure her brother could attend.

Walking into the well-lit hall, William breathed deeply, enjoying the scent of the evergreens draped across the room mixed with the smell of mince pies, savory meats and fresh rushes beneath their feet. It truly felt like the Yule and his heart lightened, finally having arrived and knowing he at least had several days to enjoy himself. Once the solstice arrived on the morrow, no work could be done until the twelfth day had ended. This meant that all the servants in the castle would be preparing all the food and making certain tasks were done before nightfall, so all would be able to enjoy the Yuletide with food, beverage, traditions, and family.

It was William's favorite time of year and reminded him of the days of his youth when his parents were alive and disgustingly in love. He and Elizabeth had been cared for and raised in a rare environment of peace and indulgence, where their mother was treated as an equal by their father. It had not only instilled within him a deep respect for women but also a standard he found almost impossible to achieve. He had wished to marry for love, but time had passed and no woman ever stole his heart. He had hoped that entertaining the idea of wedding with the daughter of a border clan laird would result in a good match, and yet, so far, everything fell far short of his expectations. Marjorie was the very worst of all and still, she clung to his arm as he stepped further into the hall.

Elizabeth had been even more stubborn than he, for she absolutely had refused to wed for love, remembering the devastation their father felt when Mother passed away. It had been a time of great turmoil, his wails of grief echoing through the halls of Dunnottar. It had concerned William at the time. But for Elizabeth, it had been a stern warning to avoid such grief in life and avoid love at all costs. She had done well, at first marrying Alexander simply for an alliance. But, when he died and she was to wed Robert next, her feelings for him frightened her, causing her to do all manner of ridiculous things to avoid the man. Now, she seemed as happy with him as their parents had been, and something in William ached for that in his life.

As the echoes of his past faded away and he was once again standing in the hall of Drum Castle surrounded by Keiths, Irvines, and Douglases, William took a deep breath and faced his reality. He was a man of great importance as a laird and Marischal, and he required an heir. No longer could he wait around for a love match. Still, anyone would do, other than Marjorie.

Elizabeth guided him toward the head table so he, Marjorie, and Archibald could be honored guests during the impending feast. As he rounded the table, he drew closer to Reginald, who was speaking in whispers to Matilda and that red-haired woman he had seen outside moments ago.

"William!" Reginald exclaimed with his usual enthusiasm. "Ye cannae get enough of the Irvines, I see."

"Ye would like to think so," he replied, patting Reginald on the back and laughing. "Ye are fortunate I have forgiven yer transgressions from the summer. Lizzie looks verra happy."

Matilda stepped forward and gave him a strong embrace before stepping beside Reginald once more. Having been his sister's maid for years and a companion who grew up with them in the castle, Matilda felt like more of a sister than a servant. "Aye, she is. Our schemes are always for the greater good, William, and they always go as planned." Winking, Matilda took Reginald's arm in hers, and they both looked quite proud of themselves.

"Well, I can only hope that I am never at the other end of one of yer games." Reginald and Matilda looked at each other with smirks, and a sense of foreboding crept up William's spine. They seemed rather smug and it made him wary.

"Are ye not going to introduce me?" Marjorie said with a bit of an edge, elbowing him in the side. He wished to shoo her away like a stray cat, to tell her to go play in the nursery with the other bairns but, instead, he took a steadying breath and nodded.

"Sir Reginald, please meet Miss Marjorie, the Earl of Douglas' daughter. She was our guest at Dunnottar before joining us for the Yule. And these lovely women are Matilda and..." William paused, waiting for the red-haired woman to remind him of her name, but the silence stretched and all he received from her was pursed lips and a raised brow.

Slowly, she turned toward Marjorie and smiled. "I am Mary."

"I kenned that," William added, feeling utterly ridiculous.

"Obviously," she replied, deadpan. Now he remembered why he could never seem to be civil with this woman. It all came back to him now. She was Alexander's lover before he married Elizabeth and carried his child. She was a maid in the castle, yet, similarly to Matilda, was treated like family. Carrying Alexander's child, she was, in fact, family now.

"Reginald, I am certain ye remember meeting me at the Beltane festival on Fraser lands the previous year. We spent much time together," Marjorie pressed, slowly moving away from William and closer to Reginald.

Now it was William's turn to be smug as his scheme to push Marjorie off on Reginald started to unfold. "She speaks highly of ye, Reg. Ye two seem to have a connection."

"We do?" Reginald eyed Marjorie while she stared at him expectantly, shuffling through memories in search of one of her. "Ah, I do remember ye now," he said slowly, but something about his tone told William that Reginald had absolutely no memory of the lass.

Beaming, Marjorie released William's arm and stood beside Reginald, staring up at his great height like a puppy who just found her new master. Matilda looked at Mary with wide eyes before giggling behind her hands. "And yer role in the castle is what, exactly? A servant by the looks of ye." Mary and Matilda narrowed their eyes at the bold lass but did not say a word. They knew better than to insult a guest of their laird's but he knew Matilda well enough to know how much it pained her to stay silent.

"I am a servant here, aye," Mary said calmly. "And I carry the laird's bastard. Fancy that."

Marjorie gasped and looked at William, taken aback by Mary's bold and scandalous confession. "She carries yer sister's husband's child? And she is still allowed to show her face here? If my husband used a servant as his whore, I would cast her out into the snow and let the child die with her." Marjorie narrowed her eyes at Mary, but all the woman did was shrug before looking straight at William with her hazel eyes.

"Ye have yerself a fine young lassie, there, *William*." The emphasis on his name was a clear signal to him that, though he had forgotten her name, she had most definitely not forgotten his. Stepping away, Mary walked over to the high table and took her seat on the other side of Robert and Marjorie's jaw dropped in disbelief.

"She sits beside the laird? He openly disrespects yer sister, Will!" Elizabeth and Mary leaned across Robert chatting and laughing, only confusing Marjorie further. "They… they…" pointing and stuttering, it was clear the young lass was thoroughly scandalized, but William had no desire to clarify that Mary carried the previous laird's child, not Robert's.

Thankfully, Reginald cleared his throat and his winning smile shone down on Marjorie, placating the lass as he took her by the arm. "Allow me to explain the situation to ye while I walk ye to yer seat."

Never had he seen Marjorie smile so widely and a sense of triumph washed over him. Let her latch on to Reginald so he could finally enjoy some peace for a while. He knew he would have to deal with Reginald's irritation later, but it would be worth it to be rid of Marjorie during the feast.

"Will! Do come sit," he heard his sister say, and he turned to climb the three steps up to the head table, pausing mid-step when he noticed the only empty seat was beside Mary, who continued to look at him with the same raised brow, amusement in her hazel gaze.

It struck him as odd that his sister would arrange for him to sit beside Mary and not Marjorie or even herself. But smiling politely, Will stepped up beside Mary and bowed once more in greeting before taking his seat beside her.

As servants began to place succulent and savory dishes on their table, the silence between them seemed to stretch for an eternity. Finally, clearing his throat, William looked at Mary. "I do apologize for allowing yer name to slip my memory."

Waving him away, Mary shrugged. "It is of no consequence, for nor am I."

"Ye sit at the high table, my lady. I wouldnae consider that of no consequence." William picked up the mug of ale before him and took a long draught, glad to finally wet his lips.

"Mayhap, but only because I am but the whore of the previous laird and carelessly became impregnated with his child."

Coughing, William choked and spit out his ale, watching it spray across the other side of the table and thankful nobody else sat there.

"Good God, ye are a straightforward woman," he choked out, banging on his chest to stop his coughing fit. Robert and Elizabeth looked at him strangely, but he was too shocked by her brazen words to bother addressing them.

"All I mean to say is that there was never any reason for me to expect ye to ken my name. I am but a servant of the house who is here because yer sister and Robert are gracious, and naught more. I ken who ye are because ye are of great import to Lizzie and she is of great import to me."

Not knowing what to say to that, William cleared his throat and took another sip of ale, this time slowly. When a trencher was placed between them, he paused, suddenly realizing he was to share with her. Of course, he was. Why was his mind so bloody addled? This bold woman made him feel off-kilter and rather uncomfortable. He did not care if she had been Alexander's lover. From what he understood of things, Alexander was wildly in love with this woman. She was no whore to the man. But, the conversation was much too awkward for him to wish to continue it.

Pulling out his knife, William cut a piece of juicy boar meat from the large platter before him and placed it on their trencher. "This looks like a fine piece of meat," William said awkwardly, attempting to change the subject. Slicing off the best part, he pushed it to Mary's side and she nodded in thanks. As the meal wore on, William was pleased that Mary spoke very little, for when she did speak, he never knew how to respond to her bizarre bluntness. It was refreshing, in a way. Marjorie was all bluster, constantly attempting to lure the next fool to her side and never succeeding. Mary seemed to prefer to push men away by being as honest as possible.

Archibald sat by Marjorie at the other end of the table, speaking as little as possible, as usual. Yet, he did not seem at all put off that his daughter had been arranged to share a trencher with Reginald, rather than the man she was meant to be attempting to woo. Perhaps the

Douglas laird was more desperate to be rid of his daughter than he was for an alliance. Deciding that suited him just fine, William continued to eat his meal while the hall grew more and more rowdy now that most had finished eating and imbibing freely.

"William, how was yer journey?" Robert asked him, and he was glad to have a conversation that did not involve awkward topics.

"It was mostly as expected for this time of year. We have no trouble with thieves, not that one would expect such a thing when traveling with more than two score warriors."

"Mostly as expected?" Elizabeth asked and cocked a brow.

"Aye, well. Marjorie was verra anxious to arrive, as ye can imagine."

Elizabeth nodded and rolled her eyes, clearly understanding what he meant. "Ye ken, Mary here used to travel with Alexander quite often and in all kinds of weather without a single complaint. Is that not so, Mary?"

Mary looked up from her trencher after doing her best to ignore him most of the meal and her cheeks flamed pink. "Aye. Well... 'tis Scotland, after all. One cannae expect much more than frigid winds and rain much of the time."

"Ye dinnae give yerself enough credit, Mary," Robert chimed in. "Ye ran Drum by yerself for two years after Mother passed and before Elizabeth arrived. Ye went with Alex to collect from the tenants and even helped to birth many bairns in the village. Ye are a tough lass."

William looked at Mary, who quite obviously avoided his gaze, then looked at Elizabeth, wondering why she was attempting to pull Mary into a conversation that she did not wish to be in.

Minstrels began to play near the hearth and William shifted in his seat, anxious to leave the hall and be done with the day before Reginald tired of Marjorie and attempted to pawn her off on him or Elizabeth tried to make him share more than he wished to. She still had not told him what great need she had of him, so he decided now was not the time to ask. What he needed was to be away from the table.

Pushing to a stand, William opened his mouth to excuse himself for the night, but Elizabeth clapped her hands and stood, as well. "Wonderful idea, Will! 'Tis the night before the Yule begins and we should all be merry and dance! Mary is a wonderful partner."

"I… well…" William looked around and saw couples lining up to dance to the music and wished to flee. Curse his sister. She knew he did not wish to dance. It was not that he did not thrive at it, for he was quite light on his feet. He simply preferred to be a spectator. Looking down, he saw Mary looking up at him, flushed with what he could only assume was the same uncertainty he was feeling. It was no good. He could not leave without being rude to Mary or his host, even if it was his scheming sister. Mayhap she felt pity for Mary, but one thing William could already see about the lass was that she was not seeking anyone's pity.

"Ye ken, I dinnae feel like dancing, Lizzie. This bairn feels like a boulder. *Besides*, William looks verra tired. I can see it in his puffy eyes."

Scowling, William felt indignation overwhelm him. The little chit was insulting him… and for what purpose? "Ye are mistaken, my lady. What ye see in my eyes is naught but boredom," he replied, hoping she felt his insult keenly. Putting his hand out, he cursed himself for being goaded into doing the one thing he did not wish to do. "Would ye care to dance?"

"Nay, but I shall either way," she replied and stood up, putting her hand in his. Her skin was warm and soft, and William was surprised by how delicate she felt.

"Och, 'tis grand. I am pleased ye two are getting on well," Elizabeth said, taking Robert's hand in hers and pulling him to a stand so they could dance, as well. "There is the matter of the mistletoe."

"What?" William crinkled his brow and looked at his sister, having no idea what she spoke of but wishing for this all to be done with.

"The mistletoe above yer heads." Pointing up to the rafters just above where they sat, Elizabeth shrugged as if she had nothing to do with its placement. "Ye ken 'tis bad fortune if ye dinnae kiss Mary now." Robert simply stood by and smiled as if he had nothing to do with what Elizabeth was playing at, yet the man did not seem at all surprised which made William wish to box both their ears.

MARY WAS GOING to poison them both in their sleep. Why was Elizabeth trying to make her kiss William and while Robert simply smiled like an arse?

"This is absurd, Lizzie. I am not kissing yer brother." She saw William stiffen beside her, likely feeling a bruise to his pride. But it was quite clear that the man did not wish to kiss her either, or dance. Elizabeth may feel sorry for Mary, but she needed nobody's pity and especially no man's kisses.

"Why is it absurd that ye should kiss me?" William asked, looking affronted, and she sighed, wishing to be done with it all.

"Are ye saying ye wish to kiss me, Will?" Mary asked, fluttering her lashes and doing her best to look like an innocent fair maiden, just as the child in her womb kicked her ribs hard, making her bite back a yelp of pain.

"I dinnae say that."

"So, ye dinnae wish to kiss me? Ye see that, Lizzie. Yer brother doesnae wish to—"

Feeling her body being propelled forward by the arm, Mary squealed as she suddenly felt herself in William's arms just before his lips crashed down on hers. Struggling to break away from his strong grasp, she couldn't help but feel the bulging muscles beneath his tunic when she placed a hand on his arm, nor the tingle that ran up her neck when he slipped his tongue into her mouth for the briefest moment before pulling away and putting a hand out to her. "Ready to dance, my lady?" A few people whooped, having witnessed the kiss, but continued their activities, understanding that a mistletoe kiss was nothing more than tradition.

"I…" Looking over her shoulder, she saw Robert and Elizabeth beaming with delight and scowled at them before turning back to face him. "I…" Now who was the stuttering fool?

Confusion abating, Mary felt irritation building and desperately wished to simply be away from William and the hall. Her lips had not touched another man's in her entire life. Alex had been her first and only kiss, and the only one she had ever wanted. He was gone. Her lips would never feel his again.

Fighting back tears, Mary clenched her fists into her skirt and shook her head. "I dinnae feel well. I wish to retire." Without waiting for a response, Mary ran down the steps and toward the tower. She did not wish to be seen or spoken to. Anger and pain collided within, making her heart ache for Alexander. A sob escaped her just as she finally reached the third floor of the tower and stopped to catch her breath, leaning against the cold stones and panting. Simple tasks were not so simple these days and all she wanted was Alex to be here to tell her everything was going to be all right. But nothing was all right. She was alone and chased away any man who so much as spoke to her.

She knew she was a bloody, stubborn fool. What was she, if not just a servant carrying a bastard child of a dead man who had once been married to the true Lady of Drum? She was nothing and would continue to be nothing. And yet, she preferred to be nothing rather than allow another man to take Alex's place and raise their child.

"My lady." Hearing a deep, familiar voice, Mary quickly wiped away her tears and sniffled.

"Please go away."

William's face appeared from the shadows and the frown he wore made her do the same. "I am sorry. I shouldnae have done that."

"Nay, ye shouldnae have. I didnae wish to kiss ye."

"I ken that. Nor did I wish to kiss ye."

For some reason, that only hurt more. So, the only other man to ever kiss her did not even wish to? "Well... I ken Elizabeth can be verra stubborn. I dinnae ken why she placed us beneath the mistletoe."

"I think I ken why, and I think ye do, as well. I will speak to her. Still, I am sorry I allowed my pride to get the better of me." William stepped back but did not leave. She saw the crease in his brow and sighed.

"I am sorry I caused ye to feel like ye needed to defend yer honor. I ken I embarrassed ye, and that is the only reason ye kissed me." William nodded and opened his mouth, but snapped it shut once more. Turning around stiffly, William stormed down the hall and entered the chamber just a few doors past hers, where he usually stayed during his visits. It was in this hall where Robert and Reginald had fought last summer when the entire scheme had unfolded. William had stormed out of his room in a rage and Mary had fought with him, even then. And yet, he could not even remember her name when he arrived. She had no interest in him but it stung to always feel like naught more than a piece of plain furniture in a corner of a room, never truly noticed or appreciated. She was used as needed, then forgotten.

The door to his chamber slammed shut with a resounding bang and Mary jumped, knowing things would only be more awkward between them by morning, but hoping she could simply go back to avoiding him the way he had hoped to avoid her.

Besides, had he not arrived with a prospective young bride by his side? The lass had much to be desired, for certs, yet she could understand his desire to push her attentions off on Reginald, who was much too chivalrous to reject her attentions.

Desperate for a good cry and a lot of sleep, Mary shuffled her sore feet toward her chamber, stopping briefly when a cramp in her womb took her breath away. They had begun to pain her more often as of late, and she knew her time to birth the child grew near.

"Have ye considered my offer, Mary?"

Gasping, Mary spun around and clutched at her chest, cursing under her breath. "Stephan, ye cannae sneak up on me like that."

Stepping out of the shadows, Stephan appeared with his long, dark hair and matching eyes, a kind smile on his face. "I apologize. 'Twas not my intention to frighten ye. I simply wished to speak with ye all evening and ye appeared... occupied."

She understood what he referred to, but she owed him no explanation. "I am tired, Stephan. What do ye want?"

"I want an answer, Mary. Look at ye. Ye are ready to have a child. Ye need a man to protect ye and care for ye. I have always wished to be that man, ye ken. I was that man once. I can be again. Have ye considered my offer to wed? I will take care of ye and the child... even if it is... *his*."

The way he said the last word made her scowl. She felt repulsion for him run through her veins. They had been best of friends growing up together at Drum, but just that. Any romantic notions Stephan had for her were not reciprocated. Despite her attempts to kindly rebuff him, Stephan was a tenacious and ambitious man. She was not at all certain if his desire to marry her had anything to do with love for her, or simply his love for power. He was a knight and respected well enough within the clan, but he always had been overly ambitious, and Mary wondered if her child was his connection to the laird. If he raised Alexander's child, he would be the father of Robert's niece or nephew. Mary refused to be used as a ladder to the top.

"Ye ken ye and I have always been great friends, Stephan and–"

"And who else is better to spend yer life with than a friend? We can be happy, Mary." Stephan attempted to take her hand but she pulled away and shook her head.

"Nay, I dinnae think we could." He repulsed her. It was not the pockmarks that covered his face from his childhood illness that he blamed every misfortune on. It was the gleam in his eye that told her he had a plan and that plan involved her child.

"Ye would rather be shamed by yer clan than marry me?" He was no longer smiling and Mary saw the true man behind the mask. He wanted something more than simply a marriage.

"The Irvines would never shame me, Stephan. Of that, I am certain."

"Och, 'tis not the Irvines I refer to, and I think ye ken that," he sneered, moving closer.

Backing away, fear enveloped her. Never had she been afraid of this man, but never had he been so bold. "Is that a threat?" she asked, trying to sound brave and unshaken. Though inside, she was quivering and fighting the instinct to flee.

"When I was abed with the pox, ye abandoned me. Ye went off with Alexander. Nothing has been the same ever since. Ye owe me."

"I owe ye nothing, Stephan! I am sorry ye had the pox. I didnae abandon ye. Ye were ill and secluded. I wasnae allowed to visit ye and ye ken that! Alexander had nothing to do with yer illness nor our friendship… which was all it ever was. I am sorry if ye thought more of it."

Scoffing, Stephan narrowed his eyes and shook his head. "Ye thought more of it, too. I ken it. Ye are lying to protect yerself, but I ken who ye are. Ye are a power-seeking whore. Ye got yerself with child from the laird and now he is dead, and ye are all alone."

Shaking with rage and disgust, Mary smacked him across the face so hard that his head snapped to the side, and she gasped, pulling away, never having hit anyone in her life. "Ye need to go, Stephan. Ye need to stay away from me and my bairn!"

Pushing past him, Mary opened the door to her chamber, pointed for him to leave and slammed it shut behind his retreating back, barring it behind her and leaning against the rough wood surface, heaving for breath and feeling moderately nauseated. Another strong pain gripped her belly and she groaned, gripping her belly and feeling it harden with the pains. Once it relented, she shuffled to her bed and sat on the edge, shaken and wishing to simply disappear, telling herself all would be well very soon.

Yet, nothing was well and nothing would ever be well again. Not without Alexander.

CHAPTER THREE

"Have ye both lost yer minds?" Storming into Robert's solar, he stared at both him and his frustrating sister, waiting for one of them to respond or even blink. But they both simply stared back at him calmly, no expression on their vexing faces.

Sleep had eluded him all night. He was torn in so many directions by different emotions. He disliked Mary for some reason he had never been able to figure out. Something about the woman chafed him. But, he had made her cry and, worse, his mere existence tortured her. She had rejected him and that thought haunted him. Why, he could not fathom. He had not wished for the kiss but once it happened, he had hoped for some reaction besides her running away to cry. It was all his cursed sister's fault for meddling and, for the life of him, he could not understand why she felt the need to do so. He'd come with another woman. Marjorie was never going to be his wife, but that was his decision to make and insulting Archibald Douglas was not a good idea.

"Have ye nothing to say?"

Stepping forward, Elizabeth rolled her eyes and he knew she was going to act as if nothing had happened. "It was naught but mistletoe, Will. It was placed all over the castle. Anyone could have sat beneath it. I would have pointed it out to anyone. It verra easily could have been ye and Marjorie, so be grateful for small mercies."

"Ye kenned well what ye were doing, Lizzie. Dinnae ye deny it. Ye kenned Marjorie would wish to sit with Reg and ye intentionally sat me beside Mary, which was fine until ye forced her on me."

"Do ye hear yerself?" Robert asked with a bit of a defensive edge. "Mary is a beautiful woman who is well respected within our clan. She was sought by many a man before choosing Alexander. She is forced on nobody, Will. Ye were damned fortunate to share her company. Get over yerself."

William scowled when his sister nodded and crossed her arms defiantly in support of her husband.

"The truth remains that I arrived with another woman and it is my decision in the end to choose a wife. Mary is heavy with another man's child and–" It all hit him at once, like a bear caught in a trap, being swept off its feet and knocked over the head. "That is the verra point, isnae it? Ye wish to match me with Mary so she has a husband to raise her child. Deny it!" A sense of betrayal washed over him as it all came together in his mind. "Ye invited me here to fool me into a match... with Alexander's mistress!"

A bang on the door behind him caused William to turn on his heels, startled by the intrusion.

"Well, at least someone has the manners to await entry to my solar," Robert said, glaring at William accusingly, but he simply crossed his arms and raised his brow. He would have manners when his sister and her husband showed some of their own. "Enter!" Robert shouted. When the door opened, William held his breath as Mary tentatively stepped forward, freezing when she saw him.

"Ah, Mary. Please come in," Robert said warmly and she did as he asked, for what William suspected was the first time in her life.

"Ye asked me to come?"

"Aye, we did. We hadnae expected William to be here when ye arrived, but it is just as well, for this involves him."

What could they discuss with her that involved him, if not a marriage match? William eyed his sister, but she kept a serious face and placed a hand on Robert's arm, not making eye contact with either of them.

"Please have a seat, both of ye." Gesturing to the large wooden seats in front of his desk, Robert took Elizabeth's hand and guided her around the other side, seating her on his lap when he sat. William grimaced at their constant displays of affection, but he did as he was asked and took a seat of his own, Mary slowly doing the same, placing a hand on her unborn child.

"Mary..." Elizabeth leaned over the desk and took her friend's hand, her eyes beseeching Mary to listen to whatever it was she was about to say. "Ye ken how much ye mean to me, to us. Aye?" Nodding, Mary sniffed and crinkled her brow in distress, taking a deep breath. Apparently, William wasn't the only one in attendance confused by the sudden seriousness in his sister's voice.

Looking at him, Elizabeth took his hand next and smiled. "I neednae tell ye how much ye mean to me, elder brother. Ye ken already how much I love ye."

"I love ye, as well, Lizzie. What is this all about?" His stomach clenched and churned. He knew instinctively that something was amiss, and though he had his suspicions, he hoped he was incorrect.

"Mary needs a husband, and ye need a wife."

The words hit him like a swift punch to the gut. Robert was a man who did not mince words, which William usually appreciated. But to discover his invitation to enjoy the Yuletide with his sister was naught more than a ploy to make him marry Alexander's breeding mistress was a blow even he had not truly expected.

Pushing away from her chair beside him, Mary shook her head, red waves of hair floating about her face, hazel eyes brimming with tears. "I dinnae want a husband!" she cried, gripping her swollen belly protectively. "I cannae!"

35

Elizabeth jumped off Robert's lap immediately. Robert came around his desk, wrapping his arms around the weeping woman as William watched on, feeling his head spinning with too many emotions, mostly anger at his sister and pity for Mary, though she would not wish for it. However, though he tried to refuse it, a sense of rejection battled within him. He understood that Mary only wanted Alexander and he did not wish to marry a woman in love with another man, yet was he truly so bad a match? He was a laird in his own right and Marischal of bloody Scotland. He could have any woman he wanted and he'd had many. There was no denying Mary was a beautiful woman, yet if she thought he wished to be saddled with another man's child and a weeping, heartbroken woman, she was mistaken.

"Look at me, Mary," Robert whispered and wiped away her tears before cupping her face in his palms. "I ken ye dinnae wish to wed another man. Mary... Alex is gone. He isnae coming back."

"Nay! Stop it, Robert! I dinnae want to hear this!" Mary tried to push away, but Robert gripped her arms and lightly shook her. Hearing a sob from behind him, William turned to see tears streaming down Elizabeth's face and he frowned, hating to see these women suffering Alexander's loss still after all these months, though he understood it well.

"He is gone, Mary! He wouldnae want ye to live like this! He wouldnae want his child to be fatherless or ye to suffer in loneliness forever! I ken this because he told me, Mary!"

"He didnae even ken he was to be a father!" She wailed and fell to her knees, holding her face. "I never got to tell him, Rob! I never got to feel his hand on our unborn child or see the look of pride in his eyes! No man will love me or this child as he would have! I willnae settle for less!"

It was too much. Too much pain and heartbreak to witness without feeling the compulsion to comfort her. Getting down on his knees beside her, William wrapped his arms around her and placed his chin on her head. He had no words to give and remembering his own father's grief after his mother died, he knew words would not matter. He had barely known Alex and it was not his right to attempt to soothe her with words. Instead, he hoped his embrace would be a balm to her soul.

"I ken that," Robert whispered. "I ken. But he told me to take care of ye. Before the battle, he sat me down and made me vow to ensure ye were always cared for. I cannae keep my promise if ye dinnae allow me. Ye ken verra well that an unwed mother with a bastard child willnae live well. Ye ken I will always protect ye and the child. But what happens when ye are gone, Mary? When I am gone? What will become of yer child?"

Looking up with red-rimmed, swollen eyes, the look on Mary's face broke William's heart as he continued to stroke her hair, not knowing what else to do. "I... I dinnae ken..." she hiccupped. "I am already a terrible mother, for I havenae even considered my own child in any of this!" Another wail of anguish filled the room as if all her pent-up grief was being wrenched from her body simultaneously, and it was all William could do to choke back his own tears.

"Ye arenae a terrible mother, Mary," Elizabeth whispered. "Ye have been grieving. Ye are allowed to love Alexander and miss him. But, Rob is right. Ye neednae love another man. But ye do need to marry one."

"I ken... I ken I do," Mary relented, a long sigh escaping her lips as a tear threatened to fall from the tip of her small, pointed nose.

Lifting a finger, William wiped the tear away and clenched his other hand into a fist, feeling like an arse for having immediately rejected the idea of marrying her. Aye, he needed a wife, but he was a laird and alliances were necessary. Elizabeth married an Irvine to end the feud between their clans, but his people gained nothing by him marrying another Irvine. Dunnottar needed a lady to run it, but more than that, it needed protection.

"Lizzie… may we speak in private?" he asked his sister and got back up on his feet. Mary looked up at him with what he assumed was a show of gratitude for his support before she crumpled into tears once more. Nodding, his sister left Robert's side and opened the door, so they could speak in the hall.

"I ken ye are angry with me, Will, but ye can see this is the best match for ye both. She carries an Irvine heir, my dead husband's child. She needs protection, Will. She ran Drum for years. Ye need a wife who can run Dunnottar and she is that wife. She already holds an heir in her womb. Ye must consider her a better match than Marjorie Douglas."

Clearing his throat, William blew out a strong breath and shook his head, running a frazzled hand through his hair. "Aye… and nay. Lizzie, ye ken I need to marry for an alliance. Love was something I had hoped to find but didnae. Ye are correct that I need a wife. Ye are also correct that Marjorie isnae a good match for me, though the alliance is. Mary, as terrible as I feel for her, is only slightly less exhausting. The lass is outspoken and openly disdains me. Furthermore, Dunnottar gains a lady, but no new alliances with this match. She is a bonnie woman, but she is in love with another man, dislikes me immensely, and surely I can find a woman who doesnae hate me, who doesnae drive me mad, to create an alliance with."

"Ye ken there are two parents involved in the creation of a child, aye?" Elizabeth tapped her foot on the cold, stone tiles and put her hands on her hips. Why did she always say the most puzzling things?

"Of course, I bloody ken that. What the devil does that have to do with anything?"

"Her mother was an Irvine and she was raised here, but her father was the next brother in line to the Hamilton seat. She grew up on Hamilton lands as a wee lass. When her father died in battle, her mother moved back to Irvine lands. Her brother, James, is both the current laird and Baron of Cadzow. She has strong and powerful ties, Will. Mary was not able to wed with Alex because his father forbade the match. She is the youngest daughter of ten children, so as noble-born as she is, she isnae a laird's daughter, has no lands to inherit, and no dowry, but she sits at the head table for more reasons than simply carrying his child. She isnae a servant, even if she insists she is. Simply put, the woman works hard to earn her keep, lives modestly, and doesnae use her kin for gain."

William stood still, stunned by this knowledge. He would never have known, and Mary certainly never would have mentioned her connections, which somehow made him admire her even more. She stood on her own two feet, never leaning on her powerful family for support. "I had no idea."

"Of course, ye didnae. She will make a mighty alliance for Dunnot-tar and be a wonderful lady. Her kin doesnae ken she is with child and she fears she will be disowned if they discover it. If she is wed to ye and ye claim the child, ye both keep her connections. If they discover the truth before she weds, I cannae say what her family shall do, or if a war between us would start."

Though the knowledge of Mary's Hamilton ties made her a more appropriate match, there was still the matter of her hatred for him. Could he live with a wife who constantly spoke her mind, especially when her mind was filled with venom or snide remarks toward him? He supposed anything was better than Marjorie, and yet there had to be an in-between... if only he had the luxury of time to discover it.

This was not at all how he expected his morning to start and, al-ready, he had a pounding in his head that threatened to make him go blind. Gripping his temples and closing his eyes, William decided he needed time to think and fresh air.

"Lizzie, this is too much. Ye ask me to wed a woman and claim her child. And if it is a son? He shall become the next Laird of Dunnottar. And what of my future sons? 'Tis the first day of the Yule and, already,

I wish to return home." His sister frowned and he sighed. "But, I shall stay. I do believe some time in the lists will ease my mind a wee bit and help me think on the matter."

Nodding, Elizabeth put a hand on his shoulder. "That child is my nephew. He may not have Keith blood, but he is our kin and has noble ties. I ken I ask much of ye, I do. But if it is a lass, then ye still must produce an heir. If the bairn is a lad, then the pressure to gain one shall already be fulfilled. Many men go to their grave unable to have an heir and would gladly be in yer place. Family is more than blood and we both ken that. Was Matilda ever treated any different by Mother or Father because she had no Keith blood in her veins?

Scoffing, William cracked a smile. "If anything, they favored the lass over us much of the time."

"Precisely. Will ye at least consider the match with Mary?"

"Have I a choice?"

Elizabeth shrugged. "Of course, ye do, but ye would be a fool not to."

"I will consider it." He had nothing else to say. Turning around, William stormed down the tower stairs, eager to round up his men and engage in mock battles until he could no longer stand.

WALKING THROUGH THE gardens during the winter was not as satisfying as it was in spring. But after that emotional conversation and the realization that she was doomed to wed a man for the sake of her child, Mary welcomed all the fresh air she could get. Her eyes burned from shedding too many tears, and her grief felt like an endless void, threatening to destroy her from within.

When the chapel became visible through the barren trees to the east, her stomach clenched. She could not bear the thought of standing before that building, vowing to honor another man. "Lady of Dunnottar." She said the title aloud, but it felt foreign and disagreeable. What was it about William Keith that left a foul taste in her mouth? He was a fair-looking man and built well, to be sure. He was powerful and seemed the gentle sort, based on how he comforted her in Robert's solar. Still, it wasn't wealth, power, or good looks that made a good husband. Though he seemed to respect and love his sister, he was also stubborn and quick to anger. He had appeared pompous during his previous visit, and Mary had avoided him as much as possible.

"Mary!" Hearing Elizabeth's voice calling from behind her, she stopped and looked over her shoulder, watching as her friend ran toward her, lifting her skirts to avoid the thin layer of snow. Mary's hem was already soaked through with the cold, but she found it quite refreshing with all the hot flashes she'd had as of late.

"Mary," Elizabeth huffed as she reached her side. "Please forgive my impertinence. I dinnae mean to upset ye."

Shaking her head, Mary continued strolling slowly toward the outer bailey, where the sounds of men shouting and metal clanking echoed on the thick air before being carried away by the persistent wind. Her hair fluttered behind her and Mary clutched her arisaid closer to her body. "I ken why ye did it, Lizzie. I have been blind. My family will be vexed if word of my bastard child reaches them. My brother has a foul temper and blusters with pride. He willnae take kindly to an Irvine making a whore of his sister."

"Ye arenae a whore!" Elizabeth chided, but Mary scoffed in response.

"I ken that well enough, but they willnae, and Stephan approached me last night, angry that I wouldnae accept his offer of marriage, called me a whore, and I am certain there was a veiled threat about my family. And, as ye said, my child willnae live a fair life if he is branded a bastard. I should have married sooner before I looked like a mare ready to foal." Mary looked down at herself and snorted. "My belly is so big I cannae see my feet, and my breasts have swollen to twice their usual size. I daresay they are as big as yers now."

"Mary, I wish ye didnae put yerself down. Ye are as bonnie as ever and many men love a fertile woman. Ye can bear children. What man doesnae desire heirs? Ye can run a castle, and ye come from a fine family. Ye have everything a man could want. Stephan is a foul arse of a man, but he is not a threat, and certain not the only man who would desire ye."

"Tell that to yer brother. He seemed verra put off by the prospect of marrying me." The bitterness in her tone was unintentional, yet she could not help but feel rejected by his obvious distress about their potential match.

"Will would make a fine husband. Ye may never be a love match, but ye ken I wouldnae wed ye to him if I kenned he would be unkind to ye."

"And I suppose that is all I can hope for now. I went from a man who loved me more than aught to a man who can hardly tolerate my existence."

Elizabeth sighed and stopped when they approached the fields where the men appeared to be sparring. Keith, Irvine, and Douglas men were scattered across the icy fields, all wearing breeches and plaids, and not much else. Elizabeth stared at Robert as he swung his sword and Mary wished to roll her eyes at her friend's obvious affections for her husband but, in truth, she was simply envious and refused to allow herself to be the jealous sort. "Mary, will ye at least consider a match with my brother? We would be sisters and ye would visit us every Yuletide! Our children would grow up cousins and be the best of friends!"

When Elizabeth placed a hand on her flat stomach, Mary widened her eyes and gasped. "Nay! Ye are... are ye...?"

Putting a hand on Mary's mouth to silence her, Elizabeth flushed bright pink and nodded. "Aye. I believe I am. I missed my courses two months in a row and I have felt wretched. But I havenae told a soul, not even Robert. 'Tis early days yet, ye ken. If disaster struck, Rob wouldnae bear the loss well."

Clasping her hands, Mary jumped up and down, feeling as if her child may drop out of her any moment, but too excited to care. "Lizzie! Och! I am so thrilled! This is wonderful! Drum shall have an heir! And, ye ken, regardless if Will and I ever wed, yer child is already the cousin to my own."

"I ken, but just think. It would be a cousin on all sides, Mary. We will be sisters. How I do wish for that."

The clanging of swords drew Mary's attention to the fields just as she heard a deep voice shouting commands from the perimeter. Swinging his sword, sweaty muscles gleaming in the light of the late morning sun, Mary's mouth dropped at the sight of William without his tunic. A smattering of light hair spread across his chest and down his abdomen, a trail disappearing beneath his low-hanging breeches that clung to his powerful thighs and, dare she say, the most sculpted backside she had ever seen. "Oh my…"

Laughing, Elizabeth swatted her. "Ye dinnae seem to mind his visage."

"Huh?" Snapping out of it, Mary blinked and looked back at her friend, feeling a blush creep over her cheeks. "I was… admiring that messenger lad that all the lassies seem to enjoy looking at. He is… easy on the eyes."

Smiling knowingly, Elizabeth nodded. "Och, aye. I suppose he is. Though I daresay he is hard to see from this distance, and with Will blocking much of him from the view."

"Will? I hadnae even seen him…" Mary cleared her throat and took a deep breath. By all that was holy. She still did not care much for the lout, but Mary had to admit seeing Will wielding his sword without a tunic was a true sight to behold. He was not unattractive.

Again, she reminded herself that fair features did not make a man a decent husband.

Elizabeth suddenly yelped and flinched beside Mary when William threw his sword to the ground and shoved the man he had been sparring with. Taking a closer look, Mary realized William had been sparring with Reginald the entire time. She truly must have been awestruck if she had not noticed Reginald before, but now that she had, it appeared the two men were no longer sparring as she noticed Reginald's sword was already in the grass as he shoved William in return, shouting something that Mary could not understand.

"What in heaven's name are those two fighting over now?" Elizabeth questioned and shaded her eyes with her hands, squinting into the distance.

"They are fighting over me, of course." Turning around, Mary followed the boastful and nasally voice of Marjorie and grimaced at the young woman who wore a fine, red damask gown that seemed well enough for the first night of the Yule, yet a wee bit fancy for strolling the grounds during the day. "It appears Reginald's affections for me have caused William to go into a fit of jealousy." Flipping her red hair over her shoulder, Marjorie scowled back at Mary and sent her a smug grin. "I saw ye kiss William last night, and I ken ye wish to capture his attention, but even ye must ken that he has no interest in a serving whore."

Walking away slowly, Marjorie held her head high and her nose even higher. Mary dearly hoped a fly flew up her nostrils and slid down her throat. Looking back at William and Reginald, they did, indeed, appear to be fighting over something of importance, as foul words drifted into the wind, and William shoved Reginald once more, Marjorie's name being exchanged between them.

Looking at Elizabeth, Mary smiled but, inside, she felt a slight twinge of rejection. She did not wish to wed with William but admitted to herself that he was the best match under the circumstances. He, however, preferred to wed the young maiden that drove him mad, rather than her, and she could not truly blame him. He was a man with power and freedom. Why ever would he choose to wed with a woman carrying another man's child?

"I believe ye shall start calling Marjorie yer sister soon, not me."

Elizabeth stared at the two men and shook her head in confusion. "Nay. There must be an explanation. I ken it."

"Elizabeth, when will ye see? I am a ruined woman. No man will wed with me, and I must learn to accept that. If ye will excuse me, I require some quiet rest before the events of the Yule begin this evening."

Walking away from Elizabeth, she was glad to see that her friend was not intending on following in her wake. Glancing one last time at William, Mary gasped and quickly looked away again when she saw his eyes following her, just before going back to arguing over Marjorie with Reginald.

They were both fools and arses. And yet, Mary felt like the biggest fool and arse of them all for ever having considered William for a husband.

CHAPTER FOUR

"YE MUST TAKE Marjorie back. I cannae take the lass anymore!" Reginald grunted as he swung his sword just as William blocked the blow.

"Take her back? I would gladly take her back to Douglas lands any day," he quipped, knowing exactly what Reginald meant, but having no intention of being saddled with that banshee's attention once again.

"Ye ken her father expects one of us to offer for the lass and it cannae, willnae, be me, William. Ye came with her. I simply entertained her to be kind and now I cannae get rid of her."

"I am afraid ye will be the man to take her then, for I am planning to offer for another woman."

"What?" Reginald scoffed and dropped his sword into the ice-slicked grass, shoving William back a step. "Who? Ye cannae!"

"Oh, no?" Throwing his sword down, William shoved Reginald back. "Who are ye to tell me what I can and cannae do?" he shouted, seeing his breath escape in wisps before drifting off into the chilly breeze. He was lying, but only slightly. Offering for Mary had not been a decision he had made just yet, and he had not been at all certain about it until the prospect of being stuck with Marjorie became a frightening reality.

"Ye cannae because ye arrived here with the Douglas lass and her insane father who brought his warriors and will hack us all down if his daughter is insulted and set aside."

"Then ye had better offer for her so that doesnae happen. I'm not the one who invited them. Yer lady did. I made no promises to her, and she has shown interest in ye from the moment she heard we were spending the Yule at Drum!" William shouted.

Reginald shoved William again and growled. "I willnae offer for her, and I willnae have a battle on my hands!"

"I will have a battle on my hands, as well, if ye havenae forgotten. My sister is yer laird's wife, and we have an agreement to protect one another. If the Douglas starts a war, he will fight us all. And I am willing to face that reality. He can find another man to wed his foolish daughter."

"Who are ye going to offer for then?" Reginald asked, his chest heaving as he finally calmed down, confusion and frustration written on his features.

William glanced to the side just as he saw Mary walking past them on the path. Reginald's eyes followed William's, and his face dropped. "Ye cannae mean Mary. Ye both cannae be in the same room without almost tearing each other apart."

"That isnae true, and I didnae say who I was offering for," William scowled. "And it isnae yer business."

"Ye dinnae need to say. I can see it in yer eyes. Ye fancy the woman."

"I most certainly dinnae. If I do offer for Mary, ye can be certain 'tis for reasons a man like ye can never understand."

"And what the bloody devil is that supposed to mean?" Reginald pushed William once more, and that was enough. He liked Reginald to a point, but the man wore on him more than Marjorie did. Pushing him to the ground, William leaned over him and clenched his teeth.

"It means I am a laird and I dinnae have the freedoms ye do to the woo lassies and live in such frivolity. I must take a wife, and I must make an alliance, and I must do it verra soon."

Pushing to his feet, Reginald wiped the ice water off the back of his breeches and picked up his sword. "Ye ken what yer problem is, William? Ye believe yerself to be the only person with expectations to meet and a responsibility to his people. Ye are self-important and a bloody arse. Ye may offer for Mary, and she may accept, but dinnae believe for a moment she does so for any other reason than necessity."

Picking up his own sword, William took a deep breath and narrowed his eyes. "Dinnae believe I do this for any other reason than necessity, as well. For that reason alone, we match well." Feeling more frazzled than he had before heading to the lists, William grabbed his soggy tunic off the ground and stomped his way back toward the keep, wishing to be done with the Yule so he could travel back to his lands and forget any of this had ever happened.

"Will!" Stopping in mid-step and groaning with annoyance, William saw his sister walking toward him with a look he knew all too well and wished to avoid entirely.

"What have I done now?" he asked, picking up his pace when she reached his side.

"What were ye and Reginald fighting about?" she asked, doing her best to keep up with his long strides.

"Marjorie," he briskly replied.

"Ye... ye are mad!"

"Ow!" Damn his sister and her ability to reach out and pull on his arm hairs every time she was angry with him. He really should have put his tunic back on before heading back toward the keep. "What the devil is wrong with ye, ye wee hellion?"

"Me?" Yanking on his arm as hard as she could, William came to a stop once more and crossed his arms. "What the devil is wrong with ye? Ye would choose that ridiculous lass over Mary?"

"What? Nay!" William replied, crinkling his nose with disgust.

"We were fighting over being rid of her. He told me I need to take her off his hands and I refused. 'Tis not my fault she attached herself to him. I didnae ask her to… though I didnae discourage it, either," he smiled and waggled his brows. "Serves Reg right for tricking us all into believing he married ye last summer."

Rolling her eyes, Elizabeth raised a brow of her own. "Ye must get over that, Will. But ye are correct. Marjorie has a mind of her own and follows any lad with a fair face. It isnae yer responsibility to woo her."

"I would thank ye for agreeing with me, but I ken ye are only doing so because ye wish me to offer for Mary instead."

"Aye. I do. She saw ye fighting with Reginald. We believed ye were fighting over Marjorie, and the lass believes ye were, as well. She is going to cause us all trouble, I vow."

William knew his sister was right. They needed to figure out how to appease Archibald Douglas, for no good would come of him being within the walls of Drum and being insulted.

"What did ye say to Reg that made him so angry with ye?" she asked as they walked through the large double wooden doors of the keep where the hearth fire crackled against the back wall and sent a welcome warmth over his chilled flesh.

"I informed him that I couldnae attempt to court Marjorie because I intend to make an offer for another woman. He was verra angry to be saddled with her, kenning I refused to steal away her attention."

"What… Will?" gripping his arm, Elizabeth looked up at him and smiled. "Ye are going to make an offer of marriage to Mary?" She sounded more delighted than he ever expected. Though trepidation filled his gut, making him feel queasy for committing openly to so permanent a decision, he knew it was the best decision to make for his people and to protect Mary while gaining an alliance with the Hamiltons.

"Aye. Ye ken it shall be a marriage of convenience, Lizzie. Dinnae get ideas in yer head. I dinnae ken if Mary will even accept. She is even more against the match than I was."

"Oh, Will!" For a slight lass, Elizabeth had strength behind her embrace that threatened to knock him on his arse. "I cannae tell ye how happy this makes me! She and Alexander's bairn shall be well cared for by a man I truly trust and ye will gain more ties to the Irvines while solidifying a strong alliance. I ken ye can hardly stand one another for now, but mark my words, ye will fall on yer knees for that woman by Yuletide's end."

"Ye are out of yer mind with delusions, Elizabeth. I will offer for her, and we will see if she accepts. Assuming she doesnae break my nose, the best we can hope for is mutual benefit and companionship."

"As ye say, elder brother." Elizabeth did not sound at all convinced, and William wished to shake the stubborn woman. For a lass who wished to avoid love altogether in life before falling for Robert, she sure seemed determined to make a love match for Will. Yet he knew it took a special bond to create what she shared with Robert and what their parents had once shared. He had hoped for such a love when he was younger and naïve, but he was too old for such whimsies. He had a clan to protect and at least Mary was not covered in pockmarks and' from what he had seen thus far, she appeared to have all her teeth. As long as her child was not born with two heads to feed, he believed this match was the best he could expect from life.

"Archibald willnae be happy when he discovers I have chosen another woman and Reginald has no interest. I am fashed about the consequences. Mayhap I should wait until after the Yule to speak with Mary."

"Nay, ye dinnae have the luxury of time. Mary isnae due to deliver her child yet, but her pains grow more frequent by the day and ye need to secure this alliance and claim her child before a Hamilton discovers she is unwed. Ye handle Mary. Let me and Robert deal with Archibald. I have just the idea to honor his daughter and stroke the Douglas ego while surrounding Marjorie with attention."

"Oh?" William wondered if Matilda's scheming had rubbed off on his sister while she had been here at Drum. "What have ye in mind?"

"We have many Keiths and Irvines here for the Yuletide and twelve days to fill. I do believe a winter tournament will entertain all the clans and the winner receives the hand of the Black Douglas' daughter."

Pursing his lips, he had to admit it was a clever plan and one that removed all the pressure on him to wed the lass. She would thrive with all the attention put on her. "'Tis a good plan if the Douglas doesnae see it for what it is: a ploy to free me and Reg of her incessant whining."

"I am most certain he is aware of his daughter's behaviors. I do believe, if we plan this well enough, he will be glad to be rid of her just as ye are."

William was not so certain, but he was willing to allow his sister to scheme this one time if it benefited him and allowed him to do what he needed. Mary came from a good family and would make a good Lady of Dunnottar. She was obviously fertile and would soon birth him an heir to claim. If it was not for the child being Alexander's, William was not certain he would be so keen to claim it, but it was important to his sister and Robert would be the child's uncle, so it was well enough to protect the bairn and his mother.

William ran a hand through his tangled hair and threw his sodden tunic over his bare shoulder, deciding it was best to find his chamber and take a bath before attempting to speak with Mary, a task he already dreaded.

Looking at his sister, William rubbed his short beard and raised a brow. "I wish ye good fortune dealing with Archibald. But something tells me I am the one in need of fortune, for I dinnae ken if Mary will accept me or injure me."

"I will ken when next I see ye if yer lip is bloodied and yer nose is crooked." Elizabeth smiled widely and bounced on her toes before walking toward the tower stairs, most certainly to find Robert's solar and start her scheming.

ARRIVING EARLY TO the hall before the evening meal was to begin for the first night of Yule, Mary stood in front of the hearth, watching the Yule log burn with flickering flames of orange and blue while rubbing her hands to warm her chilled bones. It seemed she was either on fire or half-frozen these days, and though she had a few sennights left before she expected to deliver her child, she feared it was coming sooner than expected.

Hundreds of people would be gathering in the hall soon and she had seen Cook preparing a sumptuous meal of roasted boar, pheasant, swan, and more sweetmeats, loaves of bread, and pies than she could count. The hall smelled of a mixture of herbs from both the rushes below her feet and the hanging evergreens all around. This was her favorite time of year, and yet, without Alex, it felt dreary and cheerless. Rubbing her belly, she thanked God for the miracle resting within her womb, for without their child, Mary would be truly bereft.

"My lady. May I have a word?" Looking over her shoulder, Mary saw William standing behind her, his hair still damp, and a pleasant scent of cloves lingering around him. His short beard appeared freshly groomed and his crisp tunic was covered by a fine leather jerkin with his Keith plaid draped over his shoulder.

Licking her lips nervously, Mary took a deep breath and scanned his features, suddenly glad she had put on her best gown for the festivities. Matilda had insisted she wear the emerald green silk gown provided for her, the hem let out to accommodate her swollen abdomen and the laces facing the back. The modest neckline did well enough to support her breasts since a corset was an impossibility, but she admitted that she was pleased with the fit and her hazel eyes had appeared greener than ever against the green fabric. Hair done up with intricate braids and wrapped around her head masterfully, Mary decided she needed to thank Matilda for making certain she looked like a human and not a bovine for the evening.

"Sir William," she replied, looking down to avoid eye contact. "Ye may." Her heart pounded against her ribs, not certain why he was willingly approaching her, especially after having fought with Reginald over Marjorie. If he had decided not to extend an offer of marriage to her, it would be best if he simply avoided her altogether. It was not that she pined for an offer, but after having spoken with Elizabeth and realizing her dire situation, Mary had finally realized that a husband was, indeed, necessary to keep her and her child in good graces with her family. And, while William was not a man she easily tolerated, he was her best option. If he did not offer for her, Mary would likely be matched with a less savory man. At least William was clean and had all his teeth.

Aside from a few servants wandering in and out from behind the screens, they were alone in the hall, which would serve her well when he rejected her. "Ye look beautiful."

Blinking, Mary chewed her bottom lip nervously, supposing he was using flattery to soften the blow. But her pride would not allow him to believe her fragile or desperate. "I thank ye, Sir William, but ye dinnae need to use sweet words to soften me to what ye need to say."

His features hardened and his spine straightened. He was a large man, much taller than her, and her gaze moved upward, suddenly focusing on the leaves hanging over the hearth, directly above their heads. He noticed it when she did and he cursed. More damned mistletoe. Elizabeth had made certain to cover the bloody hall in the ridiculous plant. "Ye make everything bloody difficult, do ye not ken this?" he asked with clear indignance. "I paid ye a compliment. Can ye accept it for what it is?"

"Nay, not when I ken ye are simply attempting to stroke my ego before insulting me."

"Insulting ye? I dinnae realize ye saw it that way. I willnae insult yer verra existence any further with mine. Good evening, my lady." William bowed stiffly and turned on his heels, storming toward the double doors leading outside before she could get another word in. He was certainly angry for a man who had been prepared to turn her down for a spoiled, whiny lass. Had she insulted him by not allowing him to insult her first?

Scoffing to herself, Mary turned back around to face the fire, feeling sick to her stomach and wishing she could simply stop being so confrontational all the cursed time. She was not usually this way, but William simply drove her mad and her aching ribs and feet did not help matters. She had been sleeping poorly and was moodier than usual. Still, that was not his doing nor his fault. She cursed herself for not simply accepting his compliment. No man had told her she was beautiful since Alex had passed, and mayhap hearing it from another hurt too much, reminding her that he was not here to tell her such things himself.

She was a fool. No man would warm to an angry lass and she would not warm to a woman who behaved in such a way, either. Deciding to tamp down her cursed pride and apologize for her behavior, Mary turned to follow Will but squealed when she collided with a body, feeling herself being propelled backward toward the fire.

Strong hands reached out to grab her, and she landed safely in a pair of muscular arms, feeling a wall of strength surrounding her. Heart in her throat, Mary heaved for breath as she opened her eyes, realizing how close she had come to the flames.

Golden eyes filled with concern looked down at her and she realized the strong arms that had saved her belonged to the very man she had just insulted and chased away.

"Will… I…" he frowned and searched her face, making her flush beneath his scrutiny. "Ye saved me."

"I am afraid I nearly killed ye. I am verra sorry, my lady." Still holding her in his arms, she realized how strongly she still clutched to him, but her legs shook beneath her, her body and mind still reeling from the thought that she could have been set aflame had he not reacted quick enough.

"Ye came back," she whispered.

"Aye." He hovered over her and she felt his chest rising and falling as he caught his breath and she realized he had been as frightened as she had been. It had been one second in time, but some seconds seem to last forever when the mind is fearful.

"Why? Why did ye come back?"

"Because what I have to say is of great importance and… well, 'tis bad fortune to stand beneath mistletoe and not… kiss." His mouth was close to hers, too close. She felt his warm, sweet breath fanning her face and she licked her lips, suddenly wondering why they felt so dry.

"Oh? Is it?" she asked softly.

"Ye did almost die just now," he responded.

"Aye, but only because I ran into ye."

"Still, it isnae safe to tempt fate." His lips hovered over hers, so close she could almost feel him on her. He surrounded her and, surprisingly, she was not afraid of the odd sensations he stirred within her.

"What…" she stopped and swallowed hard, finding it hard to breathe through the rapid beating of her heart. "What were ye going to say to me before I chased ye away like a shrew?"

His lips parted with a smile and she caught her breath. Aye, he indeed has all his teeth, a rare find these days. "Before I say what I wish to, I fear we are still in danger of misfortune. Mayhap we should… just to be certain…"

"Kiss?" Mary finished for him, feeling light in the head and on her feet, for William very nearly held her up by the waist as she clung to his arms.

"'Tis really the only way. I will need fortune on my side for what I have to say."

"Oh?" Mary wondered if he was afraid she would box his ears once he informed her that he had chosen to wed with Marjorie. That thought made her giggle slightly, and yet ache at the same time. She had never asked for, nor wanted, their first kiss. Yet here they were now, dancing around the next. This time, both wished for the same outcome yet were too afraid to acknowledge it.

"Well, I dare say I need all the fortune I can get." Licking her lips one last time, Mary slowly leaned in, closing the distance between them, gently placing her lips on his. When he dipped her backward in his arms, she breathed deeply and wrapped her arms around his neck to support herself. His mouth opened slightly and she followed his lead, unsure exactly how much fortune he was hoping to gain.

When his tongue gently slipped into her mouth, her stomach clenched with a mixture of apprehension and excitement. This was no ordinary kiss beneath the mistletoe. Her tongue slid against his and he groaned softly, a sound that sent a wave of pleasure up her neck.

This had been a mistake. Mary was not sure what had come over her, but William was about to tell her he was marrying another woman. And though it had been several months since she'd felt companionship or had been held by a man, kissing William was an act of desperation and she suddenly felt foolish.

Pulling away, Mary panted, trying to catch her breath while she looked down, not wishing to make eye contact with the one man who somehow attracted her one moment and made her furious the next for no apparent reason. One look at him and she may lose her senses all over again.

"Mary." Placing his finger under her chin, he prompted her to lift her head and look him in the eyes. She did as he wished and swallowed hard, preparing for rejection and wondering why it hurt more than expected to feel unwanted by a man she did not want, either.

"I would consider it a great honor if ye would consent to be my wife."

Gasping, she gripped her throat, feeling it constrict with shock, panic, grief, and relief all at once. How could so few words cause so many emotions? She had always longed to hear those sentiments, but only from one man, only from Alexander. But he was not here. William was here, and despite her attempts to push him away and the knowledge that he only chose her out of duty, she was relieved to know she would have a husband willing to claim her child and protect him, keeping her honor within her clan.

"Are ye all right, my lady?" Concern and uncertainty glistened in his honey eyes and she forced herself to nod.

"Aye. I am all right. Simply surprised."

"We both need this marriage, Mary. I need a wife to run Dunnottar and create an alliance. Elizabeth explained yer connections to the Hamiltons. Not only will that alliance benefit Clan Keith, but I am prepared to claim yer child as my own and to save yer reputation, as well as offer ye both my protection."

So, this was how it felt to enter a marriage of convenience. No romantic notions, no minced words. She appreciated his forthright nature. Though she had not known that Elizabeth had explained her relationship to the Hamiltons, she now understood why he chose her over Marjorie. Yet, that was of little consequence. She'd had love once and once was all she needed. The rest of her life would be duty, but she would have her child and a safe home. She would want for nothing. What more could an unwed woman about to birth a bastard truly expect? There would be no roses or late-night whispered words, but there would be security.

"I accept yer offer." It felt hollow and the thrill of his kiss already felt like a distant memory, a fading echo in the distance. Still, if she was married to William and moved to Dunnottar, she and her bairn would be safely away from Stephan, who she vowed watched her every move.

Nodding his head, William took her hand and squeezed it gently. "I am glad, Mary. I shall be a good husband and father. I will let Lizzie and Robert ken immediately. We will wed before the Yule is over and leave for Dunnottar when ye are able to travel."

The sudden realization that she would have to leave her home and her people hit her with the weight of a thousand boulders. She had once lived on Hamilton lands as a wee lass, but much of her life had been spent here with her mother at Drum. When her father passed away and she went to live with her Irvine kin, Alexander's father had made certain she was well-cared for until his dying day, which was only last summer. The Irvines were her family, and Drum was her home. But soon, she would have a new clan and a new home to run.

Biting back tears, Mary nodded and turned back toward the fire, too afraid to speak, lest her voice quake and betray her trepidation. She considered herself a strong woman, but even this was enough to make her tremble with uncertainty.

She felt his presence behind her for a moment, then she heard his heavy steps walking toward the tower stairs before silence consumed her once more. Her fate was sealed and though she knew it was for the best, nothing, not even his gentle touch nor his tender kisses could soothe her heart. Soon, the rest of the clan would be made aware of the arrangement, and she would be off to the secluded castle of Dunnottar, surrounded by cliffs and waves – virtually a new world altogether.

CHAPTER FIVE

ARCHIBALD SLAMMED HIS fist down on Robert's desk, the veins in his neck throbbing until William wondered if the man's head would explode. And though it would make quite a mess, it would certainly resolve many of his issues.

"This is unacceptable! Ye were courting my daughter. We were expecting an alliance! Ye cannae marry another woman!"

"I dinnae recall when it became yer right to order me about." William was finished with both The Douglas and his insufferable daughter, who had playacted with tears the moment she heard the news. "Neither of ye cared when ye hoped for a match with Reginald."

Standing in the corner with one leg propped against the wall, Reginald stood silent and calm, watching Archibald wearily with one hand on the hilt of his sword in case the man became a threat.

"Laird Douglas, we understand that ye are frustrated, but no contracts were drawn and no promises were made. Sir William is a laird in his own right, a knight of Scotland and Marischal to the king. He is certainly within his own right to choose a wife he believes will meet his needs."

"She is a whore!" he spat and William propelled himself out of his chair, starting to draw his sword.

"Ye willnae speak of the woman with such disrespect unless ye wish to meet me in the lists." Reginald stood still, but his eyes narrowed and he stared at Archibald with a look that even frightened William and he was dearly grateful to be an ally of the Irvines at that moment, for he would not wish to meet that fierce scowl on the battlefield.

"I demand Reginald offer for my daughter!" William stepped away from the man slowly but did not remove his hand from his weapon.

"Is it truly an offer if it is forcibly given?" Reginald asked coldly, not blinking an eye. "Yer daughter is a lovely woman but I am afraid I'm not in need of a wife just yet, nor have I much to offer as the youngest son."

"I dinnae care if ye are a laird or a lord! Ye are noble-born, and ye are a knight. That will do. She needs a husband and none of her suitors have given her an offer. She will be useless to me if no alliance is made!"

The man was an arse, and William felt a twinge of pity for his daughter. Standing from his chair, Robert rounded his desk and faced The Douglas with an air of calm and calculation.

"We understand that ye are disappointed not to have an offer from either man, but there are many men here at Drum for the Yuletide that would make an excellent match for Miss Douglas. The Keiths and the Irvines all have their verra best noble-born warriors, many knighted or working toward that honor, here on our lands and looking for merriment during the Yule. The weather is cold but the snow has been minimal. We offer ye the use of our lands to host a tournament. It will entertain the hundreds of kin we all have here with us, fill the days with games, and allow the men to show off their prowess while attempting to gain the hand of the beautiful Marjorie Douglas."

Rubbing his long, graying beard, Archibald seemed to calm a wee bit as he considered the offer. "I accept, on one condition," The Douglas finally said after a few awkward seconds of staring down every man in the room. "I demand Reginald and William both enter the contest. It willnae look well if the two men she hoped to gain offers from are not among her suitors. No man will enter to win her hand if they believe she has been rejected by two of the most powerful men at Drum."

William narrowed his eyes and shook his head. "Nay, I am already betrothed to Mary. I willnae fight for another woman's hand in a tournament. The entire situation is madness. It shouldnae require a tournament to find a husband for yer daughter. Mayhap ye should groom her on her behaviors instead of trying to always please her!"

He knew he was walking a dangerous line, but William was done being told what to do by this man who was no authority to him. He wished he had never responded to the missive Archibald sent in the autumn suggesting the cursed match. Marjorie was difficult at best, but she was simply a child on the brink of womanhood. This man was a grown leader who succumbed to the whimsies of his daughter at every turn. He had created a monster akin to those found in the ancient stories of Rome.

Stepping up to him slowly, Archibald put his hand on his sword's hilt and rubbed his beard. "Ye insult me and my daughter, do ye? Mayhap we should meet in the lists, after all."

"I welcome it." William was not afraid of this man. He was a Black Douglas, aye, but he forgot his place if he thought he could force his daughter upon William.

"William and Reginald will both enter the tournament. Invitations will be sent to every available knight or nobleman from both the Keith and Irvine Clans on our lands. Ye have my word." Looking over Archibald's shoulder, William scowled at Robert for interfering and giving in to this arse of a man. Nodding and sending William a smug look of victory, Archibald backed away and left the solar, slamming the door much harder than necessary. To that man, everything was a battle to be won.

"Are ye mad?" William shouted. "I willnae fight for Marjorie! Ye wanted me to wed Mary and now that I have offered for her, ye will force me to be in this ridiculous tournament meant solely to appease an absurd lass and her blustering father! Have ye lost yer wits, man?"

Reginald sighed and stepped forward, remaining as calm as ever but clearly unhappy with Robert's decision. "I suppose my time has come to disown the clan and run for the hills," he said wearily. "Ye ken I willnae marry her."

Putting his hands on his hips, Robert looked at both men with his blue eyes and lowered his brow. "I ken ye willnae. Neither of ye will. Simply lose and bow out of the tournament."

That chafed Reginald, who scoffed and shook his head. "Marry that lass or intentionally embarrass myself in front of hundreds of people? Ye ken we are both knighted and have fought in many battles! These games are already insane, and that is saying a lot coming from me! I willnae marry her, and I willnae intentionally lose any game of skill!"

"I agree," William said, this time being the calm one in the room. "Ye ask too much. Ye invited them here for the Yule, and now ye allow them to overstep."

Robert slowly stepped up to them and narrowed his gaze. "Have ye forgotten that we have scores of Douglas warriors on our land, ready to cause trouble at Archibald's signal? Have ye forgotten that he is one of the most powerful men in Scotland, married to the cursed king's sister? Or that we need an alliance with them? Marjorie is royalty, and dinnae ye forget it. Not all men are as ridiculous as ye two. There are men among us who will gladly wed a royal miss who is fair of feature, wealthy, powerful, and young enough to bear children. We cannae insult her honor, nor Archibald's."

Pausing, Robert pursed his lips and shifted his stance, popping his knuckles in anger. William had never seen his brother-by-marriage so enraged. "I am Laird of Drum, not either of ye, and I will protect my people and decide what is right. And when ye call this tournament ridiculous, ye insult my wife, who has done all she can to keep the peace."

William puffed out a breath of frustration. "Yer wife erred by inviting them here in the first place. If she had stayed out of everyone's business, I wouldnae be betrothed to a woman carrying yer brother's bastard!"

He knew he had gone too far the moment the words left his mouth, but it was too late. They had been said, and Robert's fist was already flying toward his face. He could have dodged it. But nay. It was his own cursed fault and he deserved the blow.

Feeling his head snap to the side by the impact, William stood his ground and straightened his back, wiping the blood from his lip. "Dinnae ye ever insult my wife again. Dinnae ye ever insult Mary again. Ye will wed her, and ye will respect her, or I will run ye through myself. Ye will fight in this tournament to prevent a war within the walls of Drum. Ye will set yer own cursed pride aside and lose the first bloody game and then ye will be wed to Mary immediately. Do ye understand me, Sir William?"

He felt himself grinding his teeth as his jaw clenched. Nails digging into his flesh as he clenched his fists, William took a deep breath and reminded himself that he was on Irvine lands, and Robert had made his decision. There would be a tournament and William would be in it… and he would lose in front of hundreds, taking a blow to his pride, only to be married to a woman he could not even speak to without engaging in an argument.

There was no more to be said. His jaw ached and he felt blood oozing from his swollen lip, but he refused to wipe it away. He had disrespected both his sister and future wife and deserved much more than what he had received. Nodding in understanding, William pushed past Robert and left his solar, cursing himself a fool. The first Yule feast was to be served shortly, and he loathed having to explain to his sister why he had a bruised jaw, but that was the least of his troubles.

Between Mary, Marjorie, and Elizabeth, William was certain he would lose his mind before he made it back to Dunnottar… if he made it back at all before being run through by an Irvine or a Douglas.

William was a man who, though prideful, could admit to his own shortcomings and mistakes. He had certainly made his fair share while here at Drum, but one thing he was certain of was that Mary was his best option, and insulting her made him the grandest arse in all of Scotland. No more. If he was to wed the woman, he needed to stop making comments about her child or relationship with Alexander. Though he wished not to admit it, jealousy niggled at him. She had loved another man so desperately that William knew he never stood a chance to gain her affections, not that he had ever truly hoped to. But, love was something William had once hoped for and now was forced to admit he would never have it.

William would join the tournament and he would lose, pushing aside his pride for the betterment of everyone but himself. It was against his nature to allow himself to be bested by another man willfully, but so was a marriage with a woman ready to give birth. His father had once told him life was unpredictable, and it would not do to challenge the hands of fate. And though he had refused those sentiments, believing himself in command of his own life, William suddenly scoffed to himself, finally understanding his father's words.

"Ye were right, Father. I have challenged fate, and I have lost."

MARY COULD NOT see through her haze of humiliation. Marjorie Douglas flashed her a grin so full of victorious bluster that Mary wished to shake the lass until her wee head popped off her shoulders.

"A tournament?" That was all Mary could bring herself to say. William had agreed to enter a tournament to win the hand of Marjorie. Was he addled in the brain? Mayhap he had hit his head one too many times in battle and suffered from memory loss or worse, multiple personalities. She had seen such things in her time.

"Aye. All the men at Drum wish to wed with me, especially William and Reginald who were the first to sign up. I told ye they were fighting over me. A tournament truly is the fairest way. Whichever man is skilled enough to win the games, will also win my hand. I cannae wait to see how many men desire me for a wife!" She squealed and clapped her hands together excitedly before flashing one more grin and walking toward the high table.

All the clans had gathered in the well-lit and overly warm hall to celebrate the first day of Yule, but though Mary was surrounded by hundreds of people, she felt entirely alone. For a matter of hours, she had believed herself saved from ruin, and now she stood planted in the middle of the hall feeling like a rejected, worthless woman. How had her life come to this? She was guilty of naught but loving a man... and being careless while making love to him. But Alexander had vowed to defy his father and wed her until his father died and Alex had been forced to fulfill the marriage contract between his father and Elizabeth Keith to secure peace. Nothing had been the same since and, apparently, her life would be ruined forever.

Seeing William approaching her as he worked through the crowd, Mary quickly turned and headed toward the high table, too confused and embarrassed to speak with him. She knew he would sit beside her during the meal and she would have to appear to be unshaken by the news, but she needed a moment to gather strength enough to survive the night.

"Mary!" Elizabeth called to her from beside Matilda, both standing in front of the high table, awaiting Robert's appearance. "I heard the news, and I am absolutely thrilled! Arenae ye? We shall be sisters!"

Elizabeth hopped up and down with a wide smile, taking Mary's hands in hers.

"This is grand news, indeed," Matilda said with a grin. "I am pleased I didnae need to add more mistletoe to the hall," she winked. So, it was Matilda who was behind the ill-fated kisses. She should have known, although she was certain Elizabeth had been in on it, as well.

"I assume ye havenae heard of the tournament then?" Mary asked slowly, looking at the other women and unable to share in their joy.

"Och, aye. 'Twas my idea, after all. We need to keep The Douglas happy, ye ken. Besides, who doesnae enjoy a wee tournament? 'Tis like the times of King Arthur once again! It shall be splendid, indeed."

Words escaped Mary. Had everyone gone mad? They had schemed to push her and William together, and now they had set up a tournament that Will was participating in to win a chance to wed with Marjorie?

"Mary?" Hearing William's voice approaching from behind her, she flinched and cursed under her breath.

"Excuse me. I need air." Pushing past Elizabeth and Matilda, Mary maneuvered through the crush of bodies to find her way to the screens separating the hall from the chaos of the kitchens. Servants hustled about carrying plates of food while Cook shouted orders and stirred something that smelled delicious in a pot suspended over a large fire.

The door to the gardens beckoned her, and Mary put her head down as she carefully walked through, not wishing to speak to anyone. The gardens had always been the one place she felt at ease, yet tending them had been a chore she loathed. Elizabeth gladly took over its care and it had thrived. Now it was mostly barren and covered in a thin sheet of fresh snow, and Mary cursed her thin silk dress for being of no use against the bite of winter, and herself for being foolish enough to run out in the cold without her arisaid.

Stopping at a bench, Mary looked around and breathed deeply, dismayed that she could not sit on the wet surface without destroying her gown. Matilda would be furious, though the woman did deserve it for putting Mary in this position with her schemes.

"Why do ye always run from me?"

Turning around, she saw William and frowned. "Why are ye always an arse?" she snapped back, feeling her ire pique and her patience at an end.

Stepping closer, William had the decency to look contrite, an emotion she had not expected he owned. "If Rob or Reg told ye what I said about ye, I have nay defense. I was angry and I paid the price." He rubbed his jaw, and Mary realized now in the dim light that his lip was cracked and swollen, a new scab forming over the broken flesh.

She had no idea what he spoke of but knowing he had said something so awful about her that one of the Irvine brothers felt he deserved a split lip, her stomach clenched and a wave of grief washed over her. Alexander would never have disrespected her. This man was foul of temper and too proud to be born.

"I dinnae ken, nor do I care, what ye said about me. But I do ken that ye entered this tournament to fight for Marjorie's hand, and never in my life have I met a more confusing, infuriating man! Ye deserve that split lip and more!" She started to run away, then stopped, realizing her slippers had no grip on the icy ground, and she risked harming her child if she fell.

"Aye, I do deserve it and more. I am sorry, Mary. But, I was forced into this tournament. Ye must listen."

Turning back to face him, she shook her head, choking back the tears that threatened to fall. "Nay. I mustnae and shallnae. I have listened enough. I listened when ye asked to marry me. I listened to ye and to Robert and to Lizzie about all the reasons I needed to wed with ye. Now that I agreed, ye will dishonor me by fighting in front of hundreds of people to win the hand of another woman? Leave me be, Will. I am tired and wish to be alone."

"I willnae leave until ye listen."

That was it. She was done being ordered about by this man or anyone else. She would rather be alone than spend her life arguing with this insufferable man. "Then ye may stand here and freeze to death for all I care." Stomping past him, she had no idea where she wished to go, but anywhere else was preferable to his company.

"Lizzie created this tournament, and Robert demanded me and Reginald participate. I refused. I am betrothed to ye, Mary. But The Douglas is a threat to us all and he is staying within the walls. Unless we all wish to be killed in our sleep, we must attempt to tolerate him and his daughter."

"So ye will marry us both?" Turning, she crooked her brow. "That is bold and will require a papal dispensation, no doubt."

"Mary. Didnae ye hear what I said? I am betrothed to ye. I will marry ye. I must be in the tournament, aye, but I will lose. Dinnae ye see? I am going to intentionally lose in front of everyone at a tournament I am absolutely certain I would win, so that I may wed with ye."

Throwing her hands up, she felt the need to scream in frustration. "I didnae ask ye to do that! I'm not worth yer pride as a knight. I ken that! Dinnae lose so ye can wed with a woman ye cannae stand! Be in the tournament, Will. Win it for all I care! I willnae be the cause of yer bruised pride or humiliation. Ye ken ye will be fighting men far inferior to ye in skill and rank. Ye cannae lose and risk yer reputation. Nor will I be played the fool and marry ye after ye lose in front of everyone attempting to win Marjorie! I have pride too, ye ken!"

Lifting her dress, Mary stomped away slowly, looking ridiculous as she tried to maneuver on the slippery ground. She felt as if she had been swallowed up whole and thrown into a different world where everyone had gone mad. A pox on them all.

"What will ye have me do?" he shouted at her from behind. "I can do as we both please and defy yer laird, anger The Douglas, and put everyone in danger. I can marry ye and sneak off to Dunnottar in the middle of the night, avoiding the entire mess! And then what, Mary?"

Hearing the desperation in his voice, she turned and stopped, looking at him carefully, seeing the anguish in his eyes. Wisps of breath escaped her as she heaved, the chill of the frigid wind freezing her to the bone as a shiver jolted her entire body.

Running toward her, William removed his Keith plaid and wrapped it around her body, rubbing up and down her arms to attempt to warm her. "Ye shouldnae be out here, Mary."

"I... ken..." she shivered again and wondered how much of it was from the cold and how much from her nerves. She was shaken and not at all herself. Mary hated to feel so vulnerable and desperate, yet she was both of those things, and something about William made her feel even more affected by her emotions than usual.

"What will ye have me do, Mary?" he whispered and pulled her into a warm embrace. Though she wished to fight it, she had no fight left in her and she felt protected, enveloped in his body heat.

"I dinnae ken," she murmured against his solid chest. Another shiver ran up her spine just as a strong wave of pain squeezed at her abdomen. Clenching her stomach, Mary groaned and bent over, cringing against the pain.

"Mary!" William kneeled and looked up at her. "Are ye all right? Is it the bairn?"

Nodding, she swallowed and relaxed as the pain subsided. "Aye. It has been happening more often as of late. I am told 'tis my body preparing to give birth and that I am likely further along than expected. I could give birth any day."

Standing up, William embraced her once again and she accepted it, mayhap because she needed comfort more than anything in the world at the moment. "Ye are my betrothed, Mary. I am a man of honor. I never meant to make ye feel unwanted. I chose ye. I am sorry this bloody situation has caused ye distress. Tell me what to do, and I shall do it, damn the consequences."

Standing up straight, Mary looked at Will and shook her head slowly. Some moments he made her so angry she wished to strangle him, but then he would say sweet things and speak so tenderly that she found comfort and strength in his nearness. Now that her ire had settled and she had heard his plight, Mary understood that William had been placed in a most complicated position.

"Ye must be in the tournament, William. We cannae afford to offend the Douglas Clan. They have royal ties and are capable of dark deeds. Alex had told me all about them in the past. I willnae ask ye to lose and dishonor yerself. How ye manage that is up to ye."

"Mary, please listen to me, because I dinnae wish for any more arguments or misunderstandings. I want to marry ye. I willnae marry Marjorie. Archibald Douglas already kens I am betrothed to ye. He demanded I join the tournament so his daughter wasnae dishonored and to encourage other men to fight. But he kens I willnae win and I willnae marry his daughter. I am marrying ye as soon as possible. I will lose the first game and I will marry ye immediately, before this child is born and I will claim him as my own and love him as my own, I vow. I have considered this from every angle. If I were any other man, I may balk at accepting an heir that doesnae have my blood in his veins, but I grew up with Matilda, who is the sister of my heart and was beloved of my parents. I ken that love for a child transcends tradition, and I have never been a man to follow protocol, anyhow." William grinned and carefully regarded Mary. "Do ye understand?"

"If that is yer wish," she whispered. "I want and need this marriage, William, but I dinnae want to be a burden or unwanted wife. I would rather be alone all my life than feel as if my child and I were forced on a man."

"At first, it felt that way, for us both, I believe. But now, I truly do wish for this match. I ken we seem to argue often, but I believe we are both strong-willed, proud people who need to work on speaking before shouting. Ye are smart, witty, honest, and truly beautiful, Mary. I meant it when I said that to ye earlier. I will always treat ye and our child well."

Our child. Those words did something strange to her insides. She felt knotted up and liquid at the same time. Her child would never know his true father and that reality stole her breath with its searing pain. But he could have a father, a good man who would treat him with respect and love him as his own. That was more than Mary could ever hope for in this world.

"Thank ye." The words sounded strangled as her throat constricted, tears welling up in her eyes.

Looking down, William wiped the tears that began to fall down her cheeks. "Dinnae cry, lass. All will be well." His eyes scanned her face as he held her close to keep her warm. "May I be bold in my honesty?"

Her heart pounded and she struggled to breathe, unsure what he wanted to be honest about, but knowing it had to be said. "I value honesty above all else, Will. Always be honest."

His hand, somehow remaining warm despite the cold surrounded them, touched the back of her neck and a shock ran up her nape. "I want to kiss ye, Mary. This time, without the mistletoe."

His words flowed over her like a sweet caress. He truly wanted to kiss her and found her to be beautiful. And though she had to admit to herself that she found him particularly handsome and had secretly enjoyed their previous kisses, she was not certain she was ready to accept these things as truths just yet. Alex was gone. Life moved on. Why did it feel like she was betraying him to feel lust or attraction? Marrying William for convenience was survival and naught more. Kissing him under a mistletoe because it was good fortune and tradition was acceptable enough of a reason. But wanting to kiss him simply for pleasure somehow made her feel like she was betraying a man who no longer lived.

"I..." She closed her mouth and looked down, embarrassed that she was rejecting him after he had been so kind.

"Ye arenae ready." His voice was calm and even, no accusation or hurt in his tone.

"I am sorry, William. Please understand that it isnae ye. Since we are being honest, I will say that I do wish to kiss ye, and I do find ye to be... pleasing to the eyes. I just need time. Can ye give that to me?"

His hands slowly slid down her neck and arms, taking her fingers in his. "Of course, lass. Besides, with this split lip, I dinnae think I could give ye much of a true kiss anyway." He smiled and she giggled at his crooked grin, one side of his bottom lip swollen much larger than the rest.

"Aye, I had wondered about that. It appears painful," She reached up to touch it and he winced but did not pull away.

"'Tis nothing I didnae deserve. I vow from this moment forward, I will earn more kisses and less split lips." He gave a crooked smile again and she chuckled.

"I dinnae ever wish to learn what ye said to earn it, but I do hope ye didnae mean it."

"I didnae, Mary." Lifting her hand to his mouth, he gently did his best to kiss it, and she smirked at his inability to pucker his lips fully. "I suppose 'tis best ye didnae want that kiss, after all."

Taking his hand in hers, she shook her head and kissed his cheek. "I said I wasnae ready. I never said I didnae want it."

His face grew serious and his eyes locked on to hers, making her melt all over. Even with a swollen lip, he was one of the most handsome men she had ever known. He affected her in a way she could not deny much longer if he continued to look at her with sultry eyes.

"When ye are ready for that kiss, all ye must do is take it, my lady, and I will gladly accept. Until then, shall I escort ye back to the hall? 'Tis growing colder by the moment and I am certain my sister shall be looking for us. The Yule feast will be beginning.

Nodding, she allowed William to link arms with her and walk her back to the festivities, the sounds of joy and laughter drifting to her ears the moment he opened the doors. All eyes landed on them as they stepped through the entrance, and she did not miss the scowl on Marjorie's face when she saw Mary beside William, arm in arm.

She was not certain when this tournament was to be held, nor when her wedding was, for that matter. But until William announced his intentions to marry her, she knew they had to be careful. If Marjorie discovered their betrothal, she would have a tantrum and cause trouble for her clan, and that was something Mary could not allow.

Stepping away from him, Mary straightened her features and approached the head table, prepared to feast for the Yule and pretend she was not imagining her next kiss with Sir William.

CHAPTER SIX

FRESH SNOW CRUNCHED beneath Mary's feet as she walked down to the lists arm in arm with Elizabeth and Matilda. Though it was only a thin sheet and was already beginning to melt as the sun rose on the horizon, the frigid air nipped at her nose and ears. Pulling her arisaid closer to her body, Mary heard the crowd ahead and grew anxious when they rounded the corner. Hundreds of people from all the clans had turned up to watch the games.

"How did ye put this all together in so few days, Lizzie?" Mary inquired. Irvine banners proudly whipped in the wind all around the fences that had been set up and benches surrounded the field.

Smiling proudly, Lizzie shrugged and chuckled. "When I have the proper motivation, I can move mountains. And finding a husband for that lass so she leaves my brother alone is a motivation strong enough to make me raise the dead if needed."

"I am verra glad ye dinnae raise the dead," Matilda said wryly. "'Tis only the fifth day of the Yule and already this tournament looks fit for the king. How many days shall it last?"

"We have one event planned per day for three days. Today we will see the participants promenade around the lists before the joust begins. An invitation was sent to every Irvine and Keith knight in attendance who was unwed, and Will's messenger rode like the wind to invite others from Dunnottar. I was uncertain how many would sign up, but we had many men do so. I do believe having Will and Reg participating encouraged several others."

The sound of William's name made Mary's heart flutter most unexpectedly. Aside from brief greetings and sharing a trencher at the feasts the last few nights, Mary and Will had kept their distance from one another. The desire to see him was stronger than expected, as was her discomfort about him in this tournament. The crowd was larger than expected and his honor, as well as the reputation of his people, was on the line. And he was going to lose intentionally for her sake. The thought made her feel queasy and the sudden need to seek him out before the tournament had her scanning the area for any sign of him among the participants, who all roamed within the list's enclosure.

"Have ye seen Will, Lizzie?" she asked, trying to sound casual. But when her friend's head snapped to the side and she raised her brow suspiciously, Mary flushed uncontrollably.

"I havenae. Why do ye ask, my fair maiden?"

Rolling her eyes, Mary rubbed her large bump through her blue damask gown with a slightly lower neckline than she usually wore. It tied just below her breasts so she could breathe freely, yet she felt like she would spill forth if she were not careful. "I am anything but a maiden, as everyone kens. I simply wished to speak with him before the event, 'tis all. The men are already armored and I dinnae ken where he is."

As they approached the stands, Elizabeth reached up on her tiptoes and squinted into the mid-morning sunlight, seeking out any sign of her brother before smiling and pointing. "Just there! He is wearing his best armor with our motto and the roebuck etched into it."

"What is the Keith motto, Lizzie? I never did ask." Mary realized if she was to be the Lady of Dunnottar, she would need to know these details. Mary looked at William in the distance and wondered how she could gain his attention before the event started and she was forced to sit.

"*Veritas Vincit:* Truth Conquers," Elizabeth said. "I am pleased that ye are learning all about what it means to be a Keith, Mary. As for the Irvine motto, *Flourishing both in sunshine and in shade,* I am afraid I only flourish in the sun, which is why I must seek my husband to steal his warmth." Elizabeth laughed and vigorously rubbed her hands together, blowing hot air onto them. "I see Robert at the verra top of the stands. I shall accompany him. When ye are done whispering sweet words of love to my brother, ye shall sit beside me." Elizabeth winked and Mary rolled her eyes once more. Her friend was insufferable and overly excited about the match.

Matilda followed Elizabeth up to the top of the stands and Mary turned toward the lists, hoping William would see her and approach so she did not need to make a fool of herself. When he waved at her from the other side, she knew she was turning redder than a berry in the spring, but she gave him a discreet wave back, relieved when he left his horse with his squire for the day, the lad who usually was his messenger, and began to walk toward her.

"My fair lady," William said when he raised his visor, a cheeky grin on his face that made her bite back a huge smile. "Ye look more radiant than the sun itself."

"Ye sure are a chivalrous knight," she replied. "I see yer lip has healed verra well."

"Och, aye. I dare say I may even be able to pucker my lips once again." William winked and she swore her cheeks must be redder than a rose. But somehow over the last few days, she had grown more accustomed to the idea of becoming this man's wife, knowing she was finally ready to share a kiss with him once again. Seeing him in his armor, so large and strong, made her ache for his touch, a feeling that both frightened and excited her.

"Is that so?" she whispered, "Well then, I have something to say to ye, and something to give ye." His brow rose and she opened the satchel at her side and dug out the favor she had wished to bring him, slowly handing it to him so nobody else would notice.

"Mistletoe?" In the light of day, his eyes were a light green bordering on yellow that made her think of the moss-covered rocks along the shores surrounding the river she used to play in as a child. They made her feel safe and comforted.

"Aye, well. I wished to give ye a favor, for good fortune, ye ken."

"If I am so honored as to be able to kiss ye beneath it later, then I will be a fortunate man, indeed," William said, and her heart felt like a drum pounding in her chest.

"I do believe that can be arranged, but only on one condition. I dinnae wish for ye to intentionally lose, William."

"Oh? But, I dinnae understand. I cannae win this tournament, Mary. Ye ken that."

"What I ken is that ye are the Laird of Dunnottar, a knight of Scotland, and Marischal to the king. Ye cannae appear weak to any potential enemy, and The Douglas is just that. Ye must honor yer clan and yer reputation. This tournament is for more than Marjorie. It is yer chance to show that Keiths are strong and not to be underestimated."

William stared at her silently for a moment, and she wondered what he was thinking. Was he angry at her for putting him in this position? What would happen if he won the entire tournament? She was not certain, but she did know one thing. It had been wrong of Robert to force William into this tournament, knowing he was betrothed and expecting him to lose, potentially dishonoring his clan.

"I would kiss ye right now if I could, lass. Ye havenae any idea how much it means to me to hear ye say that. Ye truly will be a great Lady of Dunnottar."

"Just be safe out there, William. And a kiss will be waiting for ye, win or lose, as long as ye dinnae give in."

Nodding, William tucked the mistletoe beneath his breastplate and close to his heart, making Mary's feel near to bursting. Her feelings for this man were frightening, but they were now undeniable.

As William nodded and slammed his visor shut, turning to join the rest of the knights in the lists, Mary watched him walk away as she made the scariest realization of her life, one she never expected to happen again in her lifetime.

She was in love with William Keith.

SURROUNDED BY KNIGHTS in gleaming armor, William touched his breastplate, cherishing the mistletoe that lay just beneath and the woman who gave it to him. Mary Hamilton was truly a special woman. They'd had little interaction during the last few days aside from shared meals. He had been busy helping set up the tournament, but in the evening, everyone came together for the festivities and he had enjoyed watching her smile and enjoy herself, finally showing who she truly was when she was not intentionally pushing him away. Somehow, he even enjoyed the idea of raising her child, even though he was not truly the father and hoped someday they would have their own.

Her words had shocked him. She understood what it meant to be a knight and a laird who had to protect his people and part of that was protecting his reputation. Once he showed weakness, he was vulnerable. Fortunately, Robert had pulled him aside the day before and shared the same sentiments, vowing he never expected William to intentionally lose. Robert also understood the games men had to play for power. He had had to appease The Douglas as the Laird of Drum, but he knew he could not ask the Laird of Dunnottar and his greatest ally to show weakness.

Not for the first time, William wished he had never entertained The Douglas and his daughter, but there was no time to focus on things he could not control. The trumpets blared, signaling the start of the tournament, and the crowd cheered. He saw Marjorie and her father sitting at the very top next to Robert and Elizabeth, but when he saw Mary, he touched his breastplate one more time and was pleased when she smiled in response. She stole his breath and he felt like a bloody fool. He was in battle armor and ready to fight, yet all he could think about was the promised kiss of his betrothed.

Feeling someone smack him on the back, William turned to see one of the Irvine knights with his visor raised and recognized him as Stephan. They had sparred once or twice in the past, but never truly talked. "I saw ye speaking with Mary. Ye fancy the lass?"

"Excuse me?" William shouted over the sound of the cheering. Had the man mentioned Mary? "What of the lady?"

"Lady?" Stephan scoffed and shook his head, "She is no lady. She was mine before she was Alexander's, ye ken. The lass has more tricks than any good whore in Edinburgh, and her child is just as likely mine as it is his. Ye can have Miss Marjorie Douglas. Mary is mine. Ye had better stay away from her if ye ken what is good for ye."

Stepping up close to Stephan, William looked the man in his brown eyes and calmly addressed him, though inside a rage burned deeper than any he had ever felt before. He wanted to snap the man in two for disrespecting Mary. "Listen to me verra carefully, Stephan. Ye should be careful who ye threaten and who ye insult. Ye dinnae ken what I am capable of and if ye werenae an Irvine, I would relieve yer neck of yer pock-riddled face here and now. One more word against Mary and ye are a dead man."

He had to walk away. Stephan would be taken care of later. For now, William had to keep his head calm. Mayhap the man was threatened by him and simply trying to rattle him. It had not worked. He was as ready for this tournament as he was for any battle and nothing the man said about Mary would make him lose his focus. He did not believe anything Stephan said about Mary, and he found he did not care even if it was true. He knew who she truly was, and her past was not her future.

He loved her. The realization nearly knocked him on his arse. Looking up at her in the stands, the concern on her face told him what he needed to know. She was aware of Stephan's desire to have her. Now, he truly wished to destroy the man. Had Stephan caused her trouble? She had not mentioned his name, nor had anyone. Mayhap he was making something of nothing, but his gut told him otherwise. The man wanted Mary, but he could not have her, and never had William wanted to run a man through more.

The crowd quieted as Robert stood with Archibald and announced the games, making a display of the grand prize, the young lass sitting beside Elizabeth batting her eyes and attempting to wave seductively. She was ridiculous, but William was certain most of these men did not care about her personality, so long as they married into a powerful family. As for William, he could not wait to be done with this tournament and share a few stolen moments with Mary.

The knights all lined up to promenade around the lists, waving and trotting with their finely decorated horses. It was all a show of wealth, power, and prowess, something William knew he had, yet was never eager to prove to others. He proved it to his king, his clan, and on the battlefield. But he had been forced to be here, so he decided to make the most of it and urged his horse forward, waving to the crowd as they hollered and cheered, ready for a good show.

Mary smiled and discreetly blew him a kiss as he passed, and his heart constricted painfully. She was a true sight to behold in her blue dress with a lower neckline than usual. He could see the tops of her creamy breasts and wondered what she would look like disrobed. The desire to lay his head on her bare abdomen and feel the child within her womb shocked him above anything else. He wanted to see all of her, love all of her, to prove to her he was the best man to care for her and the bairn and that she was beautiful and worth loving. Touching his heart, he saw her smile and blush just as he rode past her.

"Enjoy her attentions now, Sir William. She will be mine once I prove myself worthy." Stephan clanked shoulders with him and rode off to the other side of the lists and William breathed deeply, refusing to allow himself to be distracted.

Why hadn't Mary told him about this arse? Ignoring Stephan's gloating, William positioned himself with the other knights awaiting their turn at the joust. Seeking out Reginald, William moved his horse beside Reginald's and raised his visor. "Are ye going to win or lose?"

Reginald raised his own visor and his bright blue eyes rolled in his head. "Never had I thought to answer such a question. I dinnae want to wed that lass, but I dinnae wish to lose to any of these men. I ken I am a better fighter than all of them... including ye." Reginald winked and William scoffed.

"Who is Stephan?" Despite all the activity around him and the sound of lances cracking against shields, all William could think about was the man he feared was causing trouble for Mary.

"That boil of a man? He is an Irvine knight and though he is kin, he has been close to banishment more than once."

"What is he to Mary?" William would learn more about the man later. For now, he was interested only in knowing what Mary meant to him.

Reginald dropped his brows. "That is a different question altogether. I dinnae ken. They were companions as children. He became ill with the pox and was kept indoors by his mother for months. He fought verra hard to regain strength and become a knight, I will give him that honor. But he wasnae pleased with Mary's relationship with Alex. I ken he loves her, as best as an arse can love a woman, but I dinnae ken more than that. Why do ye ask? Has she mentioned him?"

"Nay, and that is the issue. I dinnae trust him."

"And ye shouldnae," Reginald agreed, pulling down his visor when his name was called up and his squire ran out onto the field. "'Tis my time to win or lose. I think I shall win, at least this round. Let the crowd see what a real man looks like."

"Ye are a bloody fool, Reg."

"Och, I ken that." Urging his horse forward, Reginald moved into the center of the lists, waving and getting into place as his clan roared with excitement. Reginald's opponent was one of the Keith knights and William suddenly very much hoped Reginald decided to win. Though his knights were well trained and he always supported them, he did not want Marjorie marrying a Keith and living on his lands.

The two men charged toward one another on opposite sides of the list and William watched as Reginald's lance crashed into the other knight's shoulder, knocking the man violently off his horse. The crowd went silent for a moment as they watched and waited to see if the fallen knight was injured. When he slowly got back on his feet with help from his squire and signaled to the crowd, everyone cheered for Reginald who was already receiving a new lance for round two.

It appeared Reginald was playing to win and William was glad of it, though he still was unsure what he would decide to do. He did not wish to lose, yet he did not wish to remain in the tournament as one of Marjorie's suitors. Let the crowd believe what they wished. He knew he was a fine warrior and need not prove it to others. War was not a game, and he did not wish to make it so.

The men lowered their visors when they were ready to charge once more and the horses charged toward one another, kicking up dirt as the sound of duel lances breaking filled the lists. Both men made contact but only one fell from his horse.

Looking up at the stands, William saw Mary and Elizabeth flinch as Marjorie covered her mouth. Turning back, he saw Reginald remaining on his horse as his Keith warrior fell once more, this time taking a wee bit longer to get back up. Just as William was about to dismount and run to his clansman, the man was able to get up with help and signaled to William that he was uninjured. This was one reason why William disliked these games. He did not need his best men becoming injured, especially for Archibald's pride or Marjorie's entertainment.

Once the area was cleared, a judge declared Reginald the winner and called William and Stephan to the tilt for the final joust of the day. He growled when he realized he was to be paired with that bastard. Slamming down his visor, William took his place at one end of the tilt, accepting his first lance from his squire and blocking out everything else around him.

When he was in position, William narrowed his eyes on his opponent, suddenly deciding there was no way he would allow himself to lose to this piece of shite who attempted to chase him away from Mary. He would lose another day. Pride did not usually control him overmuch, but he would be damned if he lost to this arse.

Stephan began to charge toward him, lance aimed high, and William urged his destrier forward, blood pumping wildly in his veins. He wished to impale this man with his lance for insulting Mary but, for now, unseating him would do. When his lance collided with Stephan's shoulder, he heard the deafening crack of wood and the sound of armor clattering. Reaching the end of the tilt, William turned his horse around and looked down to see Stephan on the hard-packed earth lying on his back with his helm lying several feet away.

"Where is my next lance, lad?" he asked his squire and lifted his visor, ready to be done with this event.

"I dinnae think ye will be requiring it, my laird." The young man's voice cracked, and William looked back down at Stephan who attempted to sit up with help but fell back once more, whispering something to his squire who immediately ran over to the judges.

One judge stood to address the crowd, and William saw that Stephan was finally standing but required the help of two other men. "Sir William is the victor!" the judge declared and the crowd roared their approval. "The victors of these events shall continue to the next round on the morrow: archery!"

Looking at the stands, William saw Marjorie standing up and scanning the winners to see who was left. When she spotted him and Reginald, she began to jump up and down and waved wildly. He groaned and turned his gaze to Mary, who still sat but clapped and looked directly at him, and his heart began to race more than it had during the joust.

"Ye ken Marjorie now believes us in love with her since we fought to win the first round, aye?" Reginald pulled up beside him on his horse and shouted over the cheering of the crowd.

"Aye. I do ken." William groaned, waving at the excited crowd, simply wishing to be done with this madness so he could get out of his armor and hopefully win that kiss from Mary... and ask her a few questions about Stephan and what he meant to her. When he looked up to the stands once more, he saw Mary being practically whisked away by Matilda and Elizabeth, striking fear into him. Was something wrong with her and the child?

Removing his helm and jumping off his horse, William pushed through the crowd, desperate to catch up to them and make sure all was well. "Elizabeth!" he shouted for his sister and saw Mary look over her shoulder with a look of horror on her face, but his sister did not stop dragging Mary away. Before he had a chance to seek out Robert for answers, Aldrich stepped into his path and stopped him in his tracks.

"My laird. There is trouble. Brian was found dead in his chamber by a servant. Robert was just informed as the tournament ended."

"Brian? How? What happened?" Brian Keith was one of his finest warriors and a good man. He also had rejected the invitation to join the tournament, refusing to attend the event altogether.

"I dinnae ken yet, my laird. I was told by Laird Irvine to inform ye. He wishes ye to meet him in his solar."

William clenched his jaw and cursed under his breath, pushing his shoulder-length, sweaty hair away from his face. Was that why Mary was dragged away? Was she in danger? Mayhap they all were. Searching the area, William caught a glimpse of Archibald Douglas leaning against the fence of the lists speaking to one of his men. When he looked up and saw William, an unsettling smile spread across the man's face. A clear warning had been sent to William, and Brian had paid the price. If you reject his daughter or insult his pride, you lose your life by the hand of a Black Douglas.

CHAPTER SEVEN

T UGGING ON THE laces running up the back of Mary's red velvet dress, Matilda grunted from the exertion. "I didnae let this one out enough, it seems. Ye are growing by the day."

"I ken that, Tilda. No need to remind me." Everyone assured Mary that she and the child appeared to be doing well, but she felt weighed down, tired, and was certain she waddled with every step. "I dinnae think we will be feasting tonight. The Keiths are in mourning and it wouldnae be right to celebrate. Even the Yule events must be put on hold."

"Aye. 'Tis an awful situation. I kenned him well from my time growing up at Dunnottar, and he was a kind, intelligent, and loyal man. Which is why he wouldnae ever want a wife like Marjorie. Ye ken, one of the servants heard Brian speaking with Marjorie in the hall the night before. She was angry that he refused to join the tournament. He called her a shrew and vowed he would rather die alone than ever marry her. The next morning, he was found dead."

A chill ran up Mary's spine and she closed her eyes, saying a quick prayer for Brian's soul. She had not known the man, but she had seen him during the feasts and knew William was fond of him. Though she had awaited word from him, William had not come to seek her out and she was worried for him. Would Marjorie or her father harm William if he rejected her again?

"We dinnae ken what truly happened to Brian, Tilda. Mayhap we shouldnae conclude anything just yet."

"We ken his throat was slit in his sleep and the last person seen speaking with him was Marjorie. A Keith wouldnae have done it and no Irvine either. It had to be a Douglas. We havenae had a murder withing these walls ever, according to Robert. I admit I am shaken and full of sorrow, myself." Matilda sniffled and picked up the comb, carefully running it through Mary's red locks. "We willnae feast, but we must still eat if we can stomach it. Cook has worked tirelessly to prepare the venison and geese for the evening. And, if ye see William, I want ye to look yer best."

"Ye are an interesting woman, Tilda. Why do ye care so much what he thinks of me? I ken ye planned with Lizzie to push us together."

Putting the comb down, Matilda sighed and came around to look at Mary with a serious look on her face and a single tear still running down her cheek. Wiping it away, she sniffled and shook her head. "I am a Keith, Mary. But I wasnae born one. I dinnae ken who my true kin are, but I do ken that the Keiths took me in as a wee child and took care of me. I was left inside a basket in a cart. No Keiths were awaiting the birth of a child. It was assumed a traveler abandoned me there. The laird at the time was Robert, William and Elizabeth's father. I was named after his wife, Matilda, whom he loved dearly and mourned heavily after her passing. He took me into the castle and allowed Lizzie's tutors and nursemaids to be my own. I earned my keep as her maid, but I was always treated like family. Will may as well be my brother. Mary, I ken him verra well and have come to ken ye verra well, also. Ye both needed a marriage. Ye needed each other. 'Tis been hard on ye here all alone. I saw the sadness in yer eyes every day. I ken ye love Alex still and ye always will. That doesnae mean ye cannae love another man, as well, and from what I see when I look at ye now... I think ye do."

"Oh, Tilda." Choking back tears, Mary embraced her friend, so unsure how she could have been so fortunate to have her and Elizabeth by her side. Before they came over from Dunnottar, Mary had Alexander and his brothers, but no true female companions. "If ye wish me to look my best for William tonight, ye shouldnae make me cry!"

Tilda laughed and sniffed back tears of her own, and Mary kissed her forehead. "I am truly sorry for what happened to Brian. I ken ye cared for him."

"Aye. I did. We all did. Lizzie and Will are surely distraught and I am certain he is ready for revenge."

A knock at the door made both women end their embrace as Tilda removed the bar and stuck her head into the hall. "Och, speaking of the man..."

Matilda stepped aside and when Mary saw William enter her chamber, her heart quickened, as did her child. It was as if her bairn was glad to feel his presence as much as she was. His face was still streaked with mud from the tournament, and lines ran down his cheeks indicating that he had shed tears recently. "Oh, William." She did not know what to do. Embrace him? Give him his space? "I am verra sorry about Brian. I dinnae ken what to say."

"I apologize for presenting myself in this condition, my lady. I havenae stopped speaking with Robert and the other men since the tournament. We cannae believe this has happened, during the Yule of all times. 'Tis what happens when ye break bread with the Black Douglases and I blame myself for his death."

"Ye cannae!" Mary cried, stepping closer to him and daring to take his hands in hers. They were large and roughened with calluses as one would expect from a warrior, but the dirt covering them did not bother her at all. The torture in his eyes broke her heart, and she wished to hold and comfort him.

"I can, and I do. If I hadnae accepted their offer to discuss a match with her, or rejected her and caused this bloody tournament, Brian would still be alive."

Matilda touched his arm and frowned. "Ye cannae blame yerself for the actions of others, Will. Ye didnae do this. They did this. They must be punished for this act."

"By whom?" William scoffed. "King James is still a prisoner of the English and the regent is as greedy and evil as they come. Archibald is married to the king's sister! There is nobody to punish them but for us," he scowled and Mary gasped, knowing at that moment that they were on the brink of a potential war on Drum grounds.

"We must stop and think clearly," she demanded. "There are innocent people who could get hurt. 'Tis the Yule. We cannae have a war."

"We cannae make them leave without insulting them and causing a battle regardless, and we cannae stay here another sennight and hope no more throats get slit, Mary! We must act!" William raised his voice at her and she recoiled. She knew he was grieving, so she would not get angry, but his need for revenge was unfounded until they knew for certain who killed Brian.

Matilda walked over to a table against the wall, grabbing the clean basin of water and a fresh linen, then held it up for William to use. Forcing a grateful smile, William muttered his thanks and eagerly dipped his dirty hands in the basin, rubbing them together before splashing water on his face. When he took the linen and dried himself, his gaze landing on her for the briefest moment, Mary felt her heart flutter. Even when covered in grime, he was a handsome man. But beneath the layer of dirt was the beautiful, chiseled face she had grown to cherish. Much like the man himself, he could hide behind a gruff, outer exterior, but Mary was quickly learning that beneath the surface was a caring, loyal, and honorable man whose good heart guided his every decision, including the one to marry her.

"I am going to go tend to Lizzie now…" Matilda stepped around William and attempted to leave, but Mary ran over and grabbed her arm.

"Ye cannae leave me unattended with a man in my chamber, Matilda. 'Tis unseemly."

Snorting, Matilda looked down at Mary's belly and crooked a brow. "Do ye wish to tell me more about what is unseemly behavior, Mary? Besides, he is yer betrothed."

"Nobody kens that!"

"The ones who matter do. I must go." Matilda shut the door before Mary could stop her. Alone in her chamber with a dirty, grieving, and bloodlusting William, Mary cleared her throat and stood still, having no idea what more to do or say.

"I am sorry I yelled at ye." William turned to look at her and she smiled, trying to lighten the mood.

"Which time?" she asked wryly.

"Every time, Mary. Ye dinnae deserve my ire. Ye are all that is good in this world."

His words went straight to her heart, but she knew he was hurting right now and vulnerable. Reading too much into it would do her no good. She knew he found her bonnie, and that was all she could ask for. Any affection could not be expected, though she shocked herself with how strongly she hoped for him to one day feel about her the way she felt about him. It was thrilling and frightening all at once, laced with grief and guilt for loving another man.

"Well, I dinnae ken about that, but I am sorry, William. May I be of any help?"

"I do ken it, Mary. I am sorry for all of this. I have brought danger to Drum. I dinnae deserve ye."

"Hush now, William. None of that is true. We dinnae ken what happened yet. There are those who are capable of such evil acts in all clans. It could have been an Irvine, as hard as it seems to believe. Even a Keith. We dinnae ken, William. And 'tis I who dinnae deserve ye. Ye are a laird, so brave, strong, handsome, and loyal to those ye love. I am naught but a servant lass who carries a dead man's child."

"Dinnae ye say that, damn it all, Mary! Ye are verra free with yer words and I dinnae ken how ye can believe such things about yerself. I see the strongest, wittiest, most beautiful woman I have ever kenned. Alexander was a fortunate man to have yer love."

Biting her lip, Mary was not certain what was happening, or how they went from speaking about the murder to speaking about love. Now felt like the right time to blurt out that she loved him, and yet it felt like the worst time ever. He was not thinking clearly and humiliating herself would only make things worse.

"What can I do?" she whispered, pleading with her eyes to allow her to help him in some way.

William took her hand in his and placed his forehead against hers. "Ye can tell me about Stephan, Mary. I dinnae ken if ye are safe here. The tournament has been canceled and Marjorie is raging in the hall. She doesnae seem to care that a man was killed. She only cares that she willnae have any more suitors. Who is Stephan, and what does he mean to ye?" She could hear the anguish in his voice, and Mary wondered if he cared for her more than she believed, after all.

Taking a deep breath, Mary licked her lips and shook her head. "He was once my best companion as a wee lass. He became ill, and I didnae see him for months. I was never allowed to see or speak to Stephan, for fear that I would catch the pox, and then he was verra weak and his mother refused all visitors. I was only three and ten when I caught the eye of Alexander. He was the heir to Drum and, though I was the niece of the Laird of Cadzow, I was not worthy of a match with him. He needed a daughter or a sister of a laird, like Lizzie. I was naught but the youngest daughter to the second in line to the seat of Hamilton. By the time my uncle passed and my brother took

MIA PRIDE

the lairdship, 'twas too late. Alexander's father had died and he was betrothed to Lizzie."

William continued to stare at her, a solemn look on his face that spoke of both respect and pain. Was it hard to hear her speak about Alexander? "But ye fell in love with him."

"Aye. I did. Not right away, mind ye. He was six and ten and was already a trained warrior and helping his father manage the lands. He was older, and I was simply taken with him. But as the years went on, aye, we fell in love. This feels odd to speak about, Will. Are ye certain ye want to ken all of this?"

"Mary…" William squeezed her hands, and his yellow-green eyes bored into hers. "I am certain. I want to ken ye. Everything ye are willing to share."

She had no idea why William seemed so interested in her past with Alexander, or why he worried so much about Stephan, but if they were to be married, she supposed it was worth discussing. He had been patient and supportive of her condition. He deserved the truth. "Stephan grew strong again and began to train as a Drum warrior. He had scars on his face from the pox, and I ken it embarrassed him, marked him as sickly, though he fought against it and earned a knighthood. However, he never forgave me for falling in love with Alexander. We were never more than companions, yet I ken now that he wished for more and blamed the loss of me on Alexander and his illness, but he never had me, William."

"And now he wishes to marry ye?"

"He does, aye. I was afraid to tell ye, and I am sorry. Ye didnae wish to marry me, I ken that. Ye offered because it was a decent match, and my family would make a strong alliance, but ye believed I had no other options. I did, just not one I would ever accept. I am verra sorry if ye feel deceived and wish to be rid of me."

"Mary, look at me, lass." Raising her gaze to his, she sighed and tried to control the ache in her soul. Speaking of Alexander hurt and always would. And yet, being here now with William and loving him with all her heart, the memory of Alexander felt more like a bruise that ached when touched and less like a gaping wound. She was healing, and William was her balm, even if he did not know it yet.

"I am no longer marrying ye out of obligation or for alliances, and I never pitied ye. I ken ye would never wish for that. I agreed because it benefitted us both. I am staying because of all that ye are… because I… care about ye." William cleared his throat and diverted his gaze to her door. "But I'm not certain ye are safe here. Stephan made threats at the tournament. He plans on marrying ye, and I dinnae ken how far he will go. Between him and the Black Douglas, I fear for ye and our child."

There were those words again. He considered the bairn his. He was a special man and she was a fortunate woman. "I have a bar on my door. I will be safe enough. Besides, Stephan is all bluster. He is harmless. Dinnae fash yerself over me."

"I will always fash over ye, Mary. Always." When his eyes searched hers and his lips slightly parted, she felt her breath catch as her hopes soared. She had not felt it wise to remind him of their promised kiss, but wanted it more than anything, wishing to comfort him and show him her love even if she was too afraid to say the words.

His mouth lowered to hers and when their lips touched, Mary reached up on her tiptoes to bring them closer together, wrapping her arms around his neck and loving the feel of his hands sliding around her waist.

"Ye ken ye drive me mad," he breathed just before sliding his tongue into her mouth. By all that was holy. Tingling all over, Mary groaned and wrapped her tongue around his, loving the feel of him, slowly moving her hands down his chest and feeling the hard ridges of muscle beneath.

"Ye have driven me mad from the first moment I met ye," she sighed when his tongue slid out of her mouth and trailed down her throat, causing delightful gooseflesh to spread across her body.

"I wish to drive ye mad for the rest of yer life." His mouth crashed back down on hers, and she was not certain if he meant his words or if they were said in a moment of need, but they sang to her soul and lightened her heart. There was a difference between love and lust and though she was certain of her love for him, new though it was, lust was surely all he felt for her in return. Still, when his hands moved to her belly and the bairn kicked his hand, the look of wonder on his face when he broke their kiss to smile was enough to make her legs buckle. One thing she could not deny was that William truly did wish to raise her child.

Nothing about their situation was certain. When they would marry or leave for Dunnottar or when this child was born, she could not say. The only thing she knew for sure was that she wanted to feel his hands on her.

Taking his right hand, Mary placed it on her breast, and he breathed heavily, moving his left hand to her other breast. He cupped their weight and kissed her neck while she tilted her head back and closed her eyes. God help her. Mayhap she was a wanton whore, after all. Nay. That was not the truth of it. She had loved Alexander with all her heart before making love to him, and she loved this man now, though she had tried so very hard to prevent it.

For Mary, this was an expression of love, and she hoped someday he would return her affections. For now, she would settle for simply feeling him, having a connection with a man for the first time in so long.

His mouth roamed lower, and when his soft lips grazed the sensitive flesh on the top of her breasts, William flicked his tongue out to taste her, and she vowed she would swoon soon if he went any further.

And then he did. Sliding his hands around her back, William pulled at the tie on her gown and pushed her long sleeves down her arms until her bodice fell below her breasts, exposing both of her rosy nipples. Reverently holding her breasts, William took a moment to gently caress them in his palms before rolling each tip into hard peaks with his fingers. "Ye are more beautiful than I ever imagined, Mary," he whispered and looked her in the eyes with a sincerity that made her love for him grow with every breath.

Bending down, he ran his tongue over the hard pebbles, sucking them into his mouth. They were more sensitive than usual, and Mary bit back a groan, feeling dizzy with the desire he was pulling from her with every caress. "Will…" she sighed his name and placed her hands on his shoulders to steady herself.

The hard evidence of his desire pushed against her belly, and Mary felt her knees go weak from the lust building in her core. It had been so long since she felt a man's hands touch her, and William's soft caresses were driving her mad with a need that had been building for so long. The need for pleasure, affection, and companionship.

"Ye taste so good," he murmured, sucking her breast into his mouth with so much eagerness and need that the sensation he stirred within her bordered on painful, yet made her groan with pleasure. "Mary…" Releasing his lips from her breasts, William trailed his tongue back up her throat and gripped her hips with his strong hands. "I want ye so badly, Mary." Pressing his forehead against hers, he groaned. "I ken I am being forward, and ye are in no condition to be intimate. But, I promised to always be honest with ye and, right now, I honestly want ye more than I have ever wanted anything in my entire life."

She sighed when she felt his manhood brush against her once more, a shock akin to lightning flowing through her. God help her, she ached to feel him move against her. It was more than loneliness, more than the need for human connection. She was falling deeper in love with him every moment and the physical connection between them had an intensity that nearly undid her. His words sparked a fire in her heart that would surely melt her from within.

"William. I want ye, as well," she whispered. Pressing her lips to his, Mary slipped her tongue into his mouth and reached between their bodies, gently stroking up the hard shaft throbbing beneath his breeches. He groaned and flexed his hips into her palm and she reveled in the knowledge that she could give him pleasure with such a simple touch.

"Ye will torture me, lass…"

"I am perfectly capable of making love, William. 'Tis not what I am fashed about. Ye are grieving right now and not in yer right mind."

Mary felt William's hand slide down her thigh and begin to bunch the velvet fabric of her gown into his hands inch by inch as he stared into her eyes with his mesmerizing yellow gaze. "I am out of my mind for ye, Mary, but I vow I am thinking quite clearly otherwise. I grieve, aye. I have much to tend to, but I have spent the past several hours raging, crying, and interrogating men. What I wish to do right now is give my attention to the beautiful woman before me, to make her feel as beautiful as she truly is. Will ye allow me to do that, Mary? Is it safe to do? Safe for the bairn?"

When he reached the bottom hem of her gown and his warm fingers grazed the soft flesh of her inner thigh, she quivered and felt her knees go weak. He was so close to where she ached to be touched. "Aye, 'tis safe, no matter what doctors will say. Men think they ken everything, but they dinnae." Mary sighed when his fingers slowly dragged along her skin. The intensity in his eyes would surely set her aflame.

"I cannae claim to ken everything, nor will I ever. But I do ken how to please ye, lass, and wish to more than aught."

"Oh?" Raising a brow, Mary smirked and felt her heart beating against her ribs. Never had she expected to feel this way about another man, to want his touch, to throb and ache all over for him, to love him so much that she found it hard to breathe in his presence. Yet, standing here with William, she knew without a doubt that she not only was capable of love and lust again but that she had lost herself entirely to this man. Somewhere between the fighting and insults, the walls between them had crumbled into dust and a profound respect and understanding had developed into a love so powerful, she was able to face the ghosts of her past, to push aside guilt and grief, and finally learn once more to live.

Her dress was lifted past her hips now, and she felt the soft caress of his touch slowly inching toward her most intimate of places. When he finally grazed her needy flesh with the barest of pressure, Mary knew she was powerless to deny him anything. He could have all of her. Mary was no innocent maiden. She understood the pleasures of the flesh, knew what was building between them, and yet it felt like an entirely new sensation, one completely foreign to her as she discovered the touch of the man she was to marry.

A sigh escaped her parted lips when William pressed the pad of his thumb against that one spot that always drove her wild and moved with gentle strokes. "William..." Knees shaking, Mary felt as if she stood at the edge of a cliff, ready to fall and shatter into pieces. And then he stopped.

Looking at him in a daze, she felt the room spin as her body craved the release it had been denied. "Why did ye stop?" she boldly asked, frustration thrumming through her.

"I want to see all of ye. Take off yer dress."

"I want to see all of ye, as well, ye ken," she responded. "Remove yer breeches, and I will remove my dress."

Wasting no time, William removed his leather belt, letting it drop to the floor, then untied his breeches, allowing them to hang low on his hips. His rod proudly sprang free just as he removed his tunic, and Mary felt her breath catch. He was a beautiful man, built like a true warrior with muscles sculpting his entire body.

The consciousness of her own body felt like cold water trickling down her spine. She had not been seen unclothed by any man aside from Alex, and never with a large unborn bairn protruding from her abdomen. She had felt like a swine for months now and suddenly worried that William would find her displeasing or worse, disgusting.

Hesitating to remove her dress, Mary gripped the fabric and nervously ran her fingers over the soft velvet. "Ye are... perfect, Will. I am suddenly worried ye willnae find me to yer tastes."

"Mary..." Lowering his brow, William shook his head and stepped up closer to her, taking her shaky hands in his. "Ye are the most beautiful woman I have ever kenned and I mean that. If ye are concerned about yer condition, I must tell ye that I find it rather excites me. Ye are a fertile, breeding woman. 'Tis a beautiful and natural thing. I do hope one day to make love while ye are carrying my child."

His soft words soothed her a wee bit, but she still felt uncertain. "My flesh isnae the same as it once was, William. I am stretched and have the scars to prove it. I fear ye will turn away." Mary wished to remain as confident as she had been a few moments ago, but the reality of her being nude for the first time in front of him with her extra weight and marked flesh made her feel less than worthy of the statuesque man before her.

Placing his hands on her waist, William began to slowly pull the dress down over her belly, getting on his knees before her. When her dress and under tunic fell to the floor in a pile around her ankles, William looked up at her and sent her a sensual grin that nearly curled her toes. "Ye were concerned I wouldnae find this appealing?" Touching her stomach, William kissed it gently before resting his cheek on her unborn child. "Ye are so beautiful, Mary." The child within decided to move at that moment, and William felt it against his cheek. Excitement filled his eyes as he looked up at her and flashed a genuine smile. "I think he has accepted me."

Emotions unlike anything she had ever felt began to well up inside of Mary. How had she pushed this man away so many times before? She had believed him arrogant, stubborn, and over-proud. Yet, she now realized he was simply confident in who he was, and he accepted her for all that she was. "Aye, I ken he does," she whispered, doing her best not to shed tears.

William gave her one more kiss on the stomach and then moved lower, softly placing his lips on the needy flesh between her thighs. A bolt of pleasure soared through her once more, and Mary groaned as his tongue flicked out. It was the slightest touch, yet her knees would surely give out if he continued while she stood before him. "By the devil, I want ye, lass." His breath was a warm caress threatening to drive her mad with lust.

Standing up, William guided her toward the bed, his eyes full of sensual promises. He looked like a lion with his golden mane surrounding his face, his short beard framing his carnal mouth. He looked as wild as she felt, and her heart raced in her chest, the anticipation both sweet and frustrating.

When they reached the bed, Mary pushed him onto his back, smirking when she saw his eyes widen with surprise. She felt free, beautiful, and full of a desire desperate to release. "Is this all right?" she whispered when she climbed on top of him, straddling his legs. "I believe it shall be easiest for me."

"Lass, 'tis more than all right. I wish to watch as ye move against me." His words were spoken so reverently that Mary bit her lower lip, feeling her need increasing with every beat of her heart. Sculpted muscles ran down his chest and Mary stroked her fingers over every ridge, enjoying the combination of smooth flesh and course hair leading down to where his manhood awaited her.

Taking himself in hand and gripping her hip, William drove her down on top of him and she cried out her sudden pleasure as he filled her entirely. A shock of lightning seemed to soar through her veins the moment they were connected. A gasp escaped her parted lips, his eyes glazing over as he watched her move. "Mary," he sighed her name and took her breasts in his palms, cupping them while she rolled her hips against him. "Ye are mine," he growled, leaning forward to take one hardened nipple into his mouth.

Never did she expect to connect with another man so perfectly, so freely. William looked at her as if she were a goddess and made her feel confident for the first time in many months. This was not simply the pleasures of the flesh, at least not for Mary. This was an expression of her love for this man, for all he had come to mean to her, feelings she never hoped to express again in this lifetime.

William thrust faster, quickening his pace and panting as he reached his climax. Mary wished to cry out, the intensity building beyond her breaking point, but she bit her lip and whimpered instead as waves of ecstasy shook her body, making her turn to liquid, collapsing on top of him. Their sweat-slick legs tangled together as she rolled onto her side, feeling William's arms wrap around her waist as he gently kissed her forehead.

Together, they lay in a tangle of limbs for several moments, silently caressing and stroking one another until Mary felt as if she would fall asleep in his arms. He was so tender and gentle, yet full of passion and strength. The words were on the tip of her tongue. More than aught, she wished to confess her feelings for him. If he did not love her, then she could bear that reality, as painful as it would be. But the need to express her own emotions felt like a demand her soul had given. And yet... fear. The fear of rejection still niggled at her mind. Could she survive it? William made her feel whole once more, yet she was still tender, still vulnerable. Mayhap she required more time to consider the words she had only ever once spoken to another.

"My sweet, I do hate that I must go. I wish to lie here with ye for an eternity. Ye ken how much it means to me that ye have entrusted yerself with me, aye?" William sat up and stroked her cheek with the back of his knuckle, a look of concern on his face. "I cannae bury myself in ye for the rest of the night, as much as I wish to. I must find out who murdered Brian."

Grief clouded his eyes as he swung his bare legs over the edge of the bed and stood, helping her rise along with him. Quickly redressing himself, William then helped Mary replace her under tunic and dress, pausing before he covered her breasts. "Ye truly are a beautiful, perfect woman. I vow we shall marry as soon as possible." William leaned in to kiss her lips, placing his hands on her breasts and making her shudder all over again with his reverent demeanor as he slipped his tongue into her mouth and rolled her nipples into hard peaks once more.

Loud shouting in the hall was followed by the door to her chamber being forcefully thrown open and Mary screamed at the sudden intrusion, covering herself as best as she could with her loose bodice, feeling mortified when a group of men stormed inside.

"Mary? What the bloody devil... so, 'tis true..."

"James?"

William jumped in front of her and she clung to his back, feeling as if she may collapse as her knees shook with fear. Her very worst nightmare was unfolding, and she was caught in a compromising position that she could never explain away.

"Come with me. Now!" James shouted, his face turning red, and tears welled up in her eyes. Humiliation and shame would be all that was left of her after this.

"Who is this man?" William asked with an edge of danger in his tone, quickly pulling a knife out of his boot and pointing it at the intruders, glaring at Robert who stood behind the man and wondering why he would allow a stranger to barge into Mary's room. Shaking his head, Robert made a face that told William he had had no choice, yet he could not fathom why.

"Tell him who I am Mary. I wish him to ken me before I gut him."

Tears blurred her vision and she crumbled to the floor, no longer having the will to fight for her pride. There was none left. "William, this is my brother, Sir James Hamilton, Laird and Baron of Cadzow."

"And who is the man defiling my sister?" James spat and stepped forward to grab Mary's shoulder, making her yelp in fear.

William grabbed her brother and pushed him back. "Hurt her again and I will kill ye. I dinnae care how many titles ye hold."

"Will… he didnae hurt me. He never would, I vow."

"Will?" James growled. "Has he a surname? A title?"

Archibald Douglas stepped forward with a pompous air. Marjorie was by his side, scowling at Mary as if she had taken a sweet treat from her collection of many. "That man is Sir William Keith, Laird of Dunnottar and Marischal of Scotland."

"Marischal?" James narrowed his eyes on William and clenched his teeth. "I ken who ye are now. Yer sister is married to the Laird of Drum, aye?" William nodded but did not loosen his grip on his blade as he continued to shield Mary. "Ye come to visit for the Yule, bringing Miss Marjorie Douglas along with ye as yer bride, then abandon her for my sister, who carries the previous Laird of Drum's bastard in her womb? Have I got my details correct?"

"Aye!" Marjorie shouted. "He was betrothed to me!"

"Shut yer mouth, lass!" Archibald roared and smacked her across the face, making her fall to the ground with a squeal of pain resembling that of an injured animal, and Mary flinched. "I have had enough of ye! I will gladly marry ye to any man at this point, even the lad who shovels the shite in the byres!"

Mary watched in horror as Marjorie's ear began to bleed from the blow, but she could not move to help the lass without exposing her breasts to every onlooker in the hall. The Douglas was truly black in the heart, and Mary felt pity for his daughter. James was angry and she was frightened what he would decide to do with her, mayhap cast her out of the clan even, but he would never harm her.

"Nay, James, that isnae the truth. William and I are betrothed, I vow!"

Marjorie gasped while she sat on the stone floor holding her ear, the red of her blood matching the silk of her fine gown, yet she still had the spirit to continue the fight. "That isnae true! He is one of my champions! Tell them, Father! He is mine!"

"Marjorie, I warn ye!" Archibald drew his hand back, threatening to hit her once more, and his daughter shrunk away, scooting back against the far wall. "He never wanted ye, ye stupid lass! Why do ye think he pawned ye off on Reginald? They werenae fighting over ye. They were fighting to be rid of ye!" Marjorie released a wail that rivaled that of a banshee's and somehow managed to get back on her feet, only to run down the tower stairs and disappear.

Lowering his weapon, William looked at her brother and spoke calmly. "Sir James. I am betrothed to yer sister. I am in love with Mary, and will raise her child as my own, I vow it on my honor. She and the child will want for naught at Dunnottar." Mary looked up at him and felt a constriction in her heart when she heard his words. Were they true, or lies to placate her brother? There was no way of truly knowing, but she prayed he meant what he said.

"What honor has a man who would plant his seed in my sister's belly and wait this long to wed her?" James seemed to be calming down, but only marginally. "Ye are the cursed Marischal of Scotland. Fortunate for ye, I cannae kill ye. I will have to petition to the regent and allow him to decide what to do with ye," he snarled.

"That willnae be necessary. I plan on marrying her immediately. I would have sooner if not for this ridiculous situation with Marjorie and the cursed tournament. The Douglas killed one of my best warriors while he slept and I willnae be going anywhere until I get my vengeance!" William spat and narrowed his eyes at The Douglas.

"What?" Archibald sputtered and turned red, stepping forward and clenching his fist. "How could I have? I was at the lists with Marjorie!"

"Then ye had one of yer men do it!" William shouted. "Dinnae ye deny it!"

"I do deny it! A Black Douglas will slit a man with his eyes wide open! Never in his sleep." The words were so forthright that Mary believed the man. He had turned nearly purple with rage at the accusation.

"None of this makes any sense!" Removing his Hamilton plaid, James wrapped it around Mary who had begun to shiver from both the draft and her shaken nerves. "If ye are the father of my sister's child, why did ye wait so long? And why did ye arrive with Marjorie? Mary is coming with me until I can figure out what to do with her... and with ye, *Sir* William. Ye willnae hide behind yer rank!" James spat at William's feet and scooped Mary up from the ground as if she were naught but a sack of grain.

All Mary could do was lean into her brother's shoulder and sob into his plaid, inhaling his safe, familiar scent and wishing she had not disappointed him and dishonored their name. She could not bear to look at William and allow him to witness the shame in her eyes or the moment of her ruination.

"Where are ye taking my betrothed?" William stepped in front of James, stopping him in his tracks. "She is ready to give birth any day. Ye cannae just take her away."

"She is no longer yer betrothed. Ye have dishonored my sister and ye are fortunate ye are so important to our king, or else ye would be bleeding out yer brains on these stone floors at this verra moment, Sir William. Dinnae ye fash over my sister. She is my blood. I shall care for her and her child and take her to a place that is safe for her delivery. She loved her Irvine Laird so well, she can spend some time with him, lamenting her sins."

Shoving past William, Robert, Reginald, and Archibald, James exited her chamber, and Mary pulled the Keith plaid over her head so the entire castle of Drum did not witness her disgrace. "How did ye ken about the bairn?" she whispered near his ear as she felt him carrying her down the spiral staircase, jostling her with each step.

"I received a missive from a concerned member of the Irvine Clan. I am grateful at least one of them has the honor to inform me of my sister's sinful behavior," he scolded.

A sinking feeling settled in the pit of her belly. Who would have done such a thing? Her shame was shared with the Irvines and everyone had loved her and protected her as family, never wishing to disgrace her and risk losing their Hamilton connections. "Who sent it to ye, Brother?"

"A man named Stephan who was concerned for yer soul. He offered to marry ye and claim the bairn, saving ye from ruin. I daresay I am considering the match even more after seeing what sort of man ye prefer to wed and what ye do with him when ye are alone in yer chamber. I thought better of ye, Mary. I thought better of the Irvines. This isnae over. I must reconsider our peace with their clan and defend yer honor."

"James... ye must listen to me. Ye are making a mistake!"

"The only mistake I made was allowing ye to stay on their lands all these years. I am going to remedy that. I am taking ye to the kirk outside Aberdeen where Alexander is buried. Ye can unburden yer sins to him, Sister, for I ken the child is his, not William's. After that, ye can stay and take the cloister, or ye can marry Stephan Irvine, the only man worthy of yer hand."

Her life was over. She was ruined, for if she must choose the life of a nun or marriage to Stephan, then she would remain at the kirk forever, alone, with only her child, Alexander's ghost, and her shame to keep her company. William would never know where to find her, nor did she expect he would try after witnessing her downfall.

CHAPTER EIGHT

"Y E'RE GOING TO allow him to walk into yer keep and carry Mary out of here like this?" William yelled at Robert and pushed him away before storming down the hall toward the stairs.

"Will!" He heard Robert calling to him and his heavy footsteps following behind, but William was shaking all over with an uncontrollable rage, fearful he may become violent if he got too close to Robert. "Will! Ye must stop."

Stopping at the top of the stairs, he turned and glared at Robert, seeing Elizabeth running toward them both from the other side. "What have ye to say? Be quick because I'm not allowing him to leave with her."

"Aye, ye are. She is his sister, William. She is unwed and he is still her guardian. He has every right to be angry, and every right to take her away. I feared this day would come the moment I learned she was with child and Alex was dead." Robert closed his eyes and lowered his head. "We failed her. This is why I needed her married!"

"I was going to marry her, ye cursed fool! And then ye made me be in that tournament and act as if I were courting Marjorie! I would have married her by now!"

"Ye are right. This ends now. Reginald, call the guards. Have Archibald locked in the cellar and well-guarded until we can weed out Brian's murderer. He cannae be trusted and has caused enough trouble. This is my cursed home and I am done trying to keep the peace with a man who cannae be trusted to do the same." Nodding, Reginald ran past William and down the stairs.

"We now have the Hamiltons on our land, along with Keith and Douglas men. I dinnae ken if we can trust the Hamiltons either, after what has happened. I need yer men to help keep an eye out for anything suspicious while I resolve these issues. We cannae afford a battle to erupt. Elizabeth, run to the village and make certain all women and children are in their homes. Then get the ones in the castle to the tower. Ye ken what to do." His sister wrung her hands nervously but nodded and ran down the stairs after Reginald.

Just before Elizabeth married Robert last summer, a group of Macleans arrived on Irvine land, including the son of the man who had killed Alexander. Fearing a violent outbreak, Robert had Elizabeth barricade all innocents into the tower while he, Reginald, and William dealt with the Macleans. That had worked out in the end, resulting in a call for peace, but William was not at all certain the same could be said of this situation.

"Where is Alexander buried? That is where he is taking Elizabeth. I must get to her!" Panic was not a feeling he was accustomed to, but the terror and angst in Mary's eyes before she buried her head in her brother's shoulder was enough to set William over the edge. Damn her brother if the man thought he would keep her away from him. He was going after her and would kill any man who stood in his way.

"St. Nicholas. 'Tis the closest kirk to here, just northwest, about an hour's ride on horseback. Go get her, Will, but ken ye will have to deal with her brother."

He never told Mary how he felt about her. All he'd had the courage to say was that he loved her. Cursed coward. He told her brother and she heard it, aye, but he needed to tell her, to make her know how much she meant to him.

"Not even the devil himself shall stop me," William said with determination. "And certainly not Sir James Hamilton."

THE CART'S WHEELS creaked against the uneven stone path they traveled and Mary cursed her brother for the hundredth time since he verily tossed her into the back. It was covered at least and shielded her from the snow falling from the dark sky. Time eluded her, but it had to be close to matins by now.

The scene in her chamber repeated in her mind and, each time, her shame deepened, sinking into her bones. She knew she was in love with William. She knew they were betrothed. There had been naught wrong with her sharing a private moment with him, at least in her own mind. And yet, to the rest of the world, she appeared to be the very whore so many accused her of being. Her brother would never forgive her.

Curse him. She did not care if he forgave her or not. If only he would listen to what she had to say instead of tossing her about like she was still the wee lassie he used to bounce on his knee then mayhap he would understand.

The sound of his horse's hooves clacking rhythmically against the uneven stones blended with those of the two horses pulling her cart, guided by her brother's trusted messenger who knew the Scottish lands better than anyone she knew. At least that was a comfort. She was certain he was riding behind the cart to protect the rear and, finally, her ire got the best of her.

Pulling the linen cover of the cart to the side, Mary stuck her head out and felt the snow falling on her head and the frigid wind instantly nipping at her nose. James lowered his head and scowled at her, before looking past her once more. "Why will ye not just let me speak?" James was being a stubborn fool and though she knew he had every right to be angry and disappointed, it was unlike him to completely disregard her.

"Ye have lost yer right to be heard, Sister."

"I willnae marry Stephan. Ye have lost yer mind! I am going to deliver this bairn any day! Please take me back to Drum, James! Please!"

Turning back to look at her, James shook his head and frowned. "There may well be no Drum left for ye to go back to when I am finished with it. Ye think the Irvines will get away with allowing their laird to defile ye, keeping yer condition a secret from yer kin, and allowing ye to remain unwed? I willnae allow it. Both the Irvine and Keith lairds have misused ye. If ye willnae marry Stephan, then ye can remain at St. Nicholas and spend yer life repenting."

Panic gripped her. She had never seen James so angry. "Ye dinnae mean that, James! What would Father say?"

"Dinnae speak of Father, Mary! He would bloody yer hide if he discovered ye carried one man's child and found ye half-naked with another man! Ye have sold yer soul to the devil, lass! I will make certain ye are cleared of yer sins before ye burn in hell."

Mary had heard enough. Spitting at her brother and missing entirely, the cart hit a bump and she yelped, feeling a pain in her womb and gripping her belly. "Are ye are right, Mary?"

"Nay, I'm not bloody all right! I am going to give birth to my child inside this cart, and if I die or lose my child, the blood is on yer stubborn hands, James! I willnae burn in hell for loving a man! I willnae! I loved Alexander! I have mourned his loss for months! Ye never wrote to me, never asked if I was well. The only comfort I had was his family! The Irvines took care of me, ye arse. They tried to make me marry, and I refused... until William."

Her voice cracked and she felt tears begin to stream down her cheeks. "I love him, James." Her brother looked at her once more and she saw the softness in his eyes before he turned to stone once more.

"Then ye will love him from afar. Ye will never see him again, Mary. Ye will take the cloister or marry Stephan and live on Hamilton lands. There are no other options for ye."

It was no use. Hopelessness was all she had left. This child would be born in this cart if they did not arrive at St. Nicholas Kirk soon. Giving up on her brother, Mary enclosed herself once more in the cart and covered her face with her hands, feeling herself crumble to pieces. "Oh, Alexander. How did I end up here?"

Though the hay beneath her felt abrasive on her flesh, the rocking of the cart and the stinging of her tired eyes soon had her eyes fluttering shut. If she fell asleep, at least she would be out of her misery until they arrived. Laying back, Mary shoved James' plaid beneath her neck and wrapped the remaining wool fabric around her body to stave off the chill that seeped into her flesh. Closing her eyes, she allowed sleep to pull her away from her pathetic reality.

Unsure how much time had passed, Mary sat up and rubbed her aching backside when the cart came to a sudden stop. The cover was pushed aside and James climbed up the back, putting his hand out to her. "We are here."

Smacking his hand away, Mary pushed herself to her feet. "I dinnae want yer help."

"Ye dinnae want it, but ye will need it."

Scoffing, Mary shook her head and swung a leg over the edge of the cart. "I need nothing from ye. Ye have done enough." James frowned and crossed his arms as he watched her awkwardly swing her other leg over the edge and feel around with her foot until she felt the solid lip of the wooden edge beneath her thin slippers.

Carefully stepping down, she winced when a splinter pierced her middle finger but refused to give up. "Ye have always been a stubborn lass, Mary."

"Thank ye." Landing both feet on the ground safely, she adjusted her skirts and scowled at her brother.

"I wasnae complimenting ye."

"Well, I take it as one, nonetheless." Not waiting for him to escort her, Mary looked up at the towering kirk walls, already hundreds of years old and built out of solid wood in an early gothic style that felt foreboding, yet breathtaking. The bell tower seemed to disappear in the haze of low clouds and the blur of snow, adding to its intimidating presence. Alexander was buried here. A chill unlike any other she had ever felt flowed up her body, starting at her toes and prickling up to her scalp.

"I... I cannae." Mary started to turn away, but James grabbed her and hugged her close to his body.

"Ye must, Mary."

Shaking her head, she looked up at James' towering height and grimaced. "Why? Why are ye doing this to me? 'Tis cruel."

Sighing, James kissed the top of her forehead. "Ye ken why I must. Ye cannae stay at Drum. Ye heard Robert. A man was killed. This is the closest kirk. Ye must stay here to remain safe."

"I was safe with William!" she cried. "I cannae be here. Alexander..." she hiccupped and tears fell down her face as snow fell into her hair. "I willnae go in. I willnae give birth alone!" The thoughts of dying in childbirth without Elizabeth by her side to aid the delivery and never seeing William again made panic rise into her throat.

"Ye carry his bairn. He is here in spirit. Speak to him. Think about what I offered. Ye can marry Stephan and come home with me to Cadzow, but ye will never see Drum again after all I have learned. I must leave. There is much to resolve, but I shall be back before ye birth yer bairn. 'Tis not but an hour's journey. Take this time alone to consider yer path, Mary."

"Why do ye think Stephan wrote to ye? Have ye no sense? He

wasnae concerned for me. He has been wanting to marry me for years and hated Alex. This was his chance! He ruined me intentionally, brought ye to Drum to force ye to wed me to him."

"At this point, I dinnae care what his motivation was, Mary!" James roared, and she pulled away from his embrace, turning around so he could not see the agony he caused her. "He is a man willing to marry ye who hasnae defiled ye before my eyes! Can ye give me one reason why Stephan isnae fit to wed ye? He is a knight. He hasnae harmed ye. He hasnae touched ye. He isnae a traitor. He loves ye and wishes to care for ye. How ye feel about him or what he looks like doesnae concern me. Ye will come back to Cadzow with him and yer child, and ye can sleep in separate rooms for all I care! But unless ye marry him, ye will join the priory here and yer child will be raised in Hamilton lands."

Gasping, Mary felt her knees go weak as her heart shattered into pieces. She would not, could not, allow her child to be separated from her. James was being unusually stern, though deep down, she understood why he was forcing her hand. He knew she would never allow her child to be taken away from her. Was this her fate? To marry Stephan and never see William or Elizabeth and the rest of the Irvines again?

She could not look at her brother. She refused to allow him to see her tears. "Go, James. But ken this: if ye hurt William or anyone at Drum, I will never lay eyes upon ye again. I will hate ye with every piece of my soul. They are good people. They are our family. Dinnae ye forget that Mother was an Irvine and even if ye stayed on Hamilton lands after Father passed, yer blood is still their own. The only person living who should atone for my deeds is me."

Looking over her shoulder, she narrowed her eyes in warning. "Elizabeth carries Robert's child. Touch either of them, and ye will be the one burning in hell." Looking back at the kirk, Mary took a fortifying breath and stepped forward, the snow falling at her feet making her flesh feel numb. If only she could numb her heart and make the pain subside.

She was trapped and her brother was her captor. She would marry Stephan. She would return to Cadzow and ache every day of her life for the two loves she had lost in this life but be grateful that she'd had them once. Never would she allow a man to take her child, but she knew they would do so, especially if she birthed a son.

"Mary." Putting a hand up to silence him as she continued to walk away, Mary refused to look upon his face. He had destroyed her chance at happiness.

When she approached the entry to the kirk, another chill ran up her spine. The doors were securely locked, and she lifted the large metal knocker, slamming it against the rough wooden surface. When she heard keys clinking on the other side before a priest slowly opened the door, a wave of nausea washed over her. How long would she be here? William would not know where to find her and after all James had said, would he even want to?

With her pains coming several times a day, Mary knew she had little time before her bairn was ready to arrive and prayed she would not be alone within these walls with only a prioress to assist in what they would consider her sinful condition. A void of emptiness made her world turn as dark as a moonless night, with no hope or light to guide her way.

"May I help ye, child?" the elderly man asked and looked at her belly, though she was relieved to see no condemnation in his eyes.

"I am Sir James Hamilton, Laird of Cadzow. My sister seeks sanctuary here." James stepped up behind her and she jumped, having expected him to have left by now. "No man shall visit her until I arrive, especially Sir William Keith, Laird of Dunnottar. If he arrives, ye are to demand that she isnae here and send word to Drum Castle, where I shall remain until I return for her."

The priest frowned and looked between her and James before

nodding and moving aside to allow her entrance. Mary supposed this situation was not all that uncommon. They likely received unwed expectant mothers or women in danger often.

"As ye say," the priest responded and gently touched her on the shoulder as she entered. She wished to spit more venom at James, but it was of no use. He would not relent in his pursuit to seek justice on those who were innocent and give favors to those who did not deserve them, despite her pleas. "Will she be taking the veil?"

James looked at her before replying. "That is for her to decide." Mary turned away from him and crossed her arms in defiance. She would not let him see her cry. Curse him.

"Mary, I shall return as soon as I am able. I expect yer decision by then. If ye choose marriage, I will deliver Stephan to ye and then travel with ye back to Cadzow. I do hope ye choose wisely."

"Have ye even given me a choice?" She could not keep her silence. He had threatened to take her child away if she did not marry. He knew she would never accept such a fate.

"Aye, I have. Ye caused this, Mary. I am simply fixing it." Walking over to her, James placed his large hands on her shoulders. They were once a comfort to her, but now they made her wish to recoil. Kissing her forehead, James looked down at her with his large hazel eyes, his dark brown, shoulder-length hair partially draped over his face. "Ye ken how much I love ye. Dinnae ye hate me, Sister. I have seen what an unwed mother goes through in this world, and I ken what becomes of those labeled as bastards. I hope ye will forgive me someday."

"How can I?" she whispered through her clenched teeth. "I told ye. I am in love with William. He is a good man, James. Tell me ye never did to another woman what ye saw him doing to me. And if ye do, I will ken ye are lying. Does loving the woman he is betrothed to make William a threat to ye? Why? Because ye never truly loved another woman in all yer life, and yet, I ken ye have done much darker deeds in yer chamber."

"Mary! Haud yer wheesht! This is a kirk! Have ye no respect?"

"Dinnae try to silence me! Ye are wrong in this! We are betrothed and he told ye he loves me and wishes to claim the child. Why must ye make me suffer? I have already suffered a lifetime's worth of pain after losing Alexander. And now ye send me here where I ken his body lies, with his child kicking at my ribs while ye threaten to take me away from my bairn or force me to wed a man I dinnae wish to wed nor do I trust! Ye say those are my only options, but they are the only options ye gave me. I have another option, James! I wish to marry William and live with him at Dunnottar as their lady. He can protect me better than a landless knight with only his own ambitions in mind! Ye are being a stubborn arse and, nay, if ye dinnae consider my desires in this and force my hand, I shall never forgive ye!"

Tearing his Hamilton plaid off her shoulders, Mary threw it in his face. "I am no longer a Hamilton. My kin are those who care for me and protect me! I havenae heard from ye in over a year. Ye ken why the Irvines didnae tell ye about the bairn? They were protecting me from *ye*, James! From... *this!*" Mary spun in a circle with her arms out in the echoing chill of the kirk's entrance while the priest watched on with a gaping mouth. She was past caring. If she was to live a life of misery, it may as well begin now. "Go now, James. Leave me in peace. But remember what I told ye. If ye harm the Irvines, I will never speak to ye again! I will make yer life one long misery, as ye will have made mine."

Storming away, Mary was not at all certain where she was headed, nor did she care. She had said all she had to say and though she knew James loved her and was attempting to protect her, he was only causing her more harm than any man ever had.

Mary heard James' footsteps departing through the kirk entrance, its doors slamming shut behind him, and she stiffened her back.

Hearing a throat clear, Mary turned to look at the priest, who, to her surprise, did not appear offended. Hands folded before him, he nodded his balding head. "I will seek out the prioress, and she will help ye to yer room."

"I am sorry for my behavior, Father." She felt shame course through her. It seemed sin after sin was compiling upon her soul.

"Ye arenae the first woman to come through these doors for these reasons, child. 'Tis not my place to judge. I hope ye will find our place of worship is a comfort to yer soul and a place to be unburdened until yer brother arrives for ye." Nodding once more, the priest shuffled his feet across the solid, dark stone floors and disappeared around the corner.

She had no idea how long she would be here, but knowing she was so close to Alexander, yet so far away, made Mary queasy. There would come a moment before she left this place where she would need the courage to seek out his effigy and make peace with her past. For now, she waited in the cold hall without a plaid to keep her warm, staring up at the towering beamed ceiling and inspecting the ancient architecture of a place that had seen more heartache and death than she ever would. Mayhap she could learn something from this kirk.

Life moved on. People died, and bairns were born. The world did not cease to exist simply because a man does. Enough time had been spent reliving the past, grieving over the loss of a future that would never exist. But, she did. Mary lived on, as would Alexander's child. And the time to face her past and move forward was before her whether she was ready or not.

Chapter Nine

HE WAS TOO far behind. William cursed into the freezing night as snow fell all around, urging his horse on. Once he and his men had swept the castle and rounded up all the Douglases into the cellar with their laird, the Hamiltons being forced to remain in the hall, William knew he would not beat James and Mary to the kirk.

There were too many threats within the walls of Drum: a dead Keith, an imprisoned Douglas, angry Hamiltons, and a missing Irvine. Stephan was nowhere to be found, and William's gut was never wrong. He had something to do with the missive James received and for the appearance of the Hamilton warriors. It was not a coincidence that Stephan had been threatening William at the tournament, confident that he would have Mary as his own. But where would the man be?

Before leaving Drum, William commanded his men to guard all the entrances in and out of the castle to prevent anyone from leaving or entering while the Irvines watched the men in the cellar. None of this would be good for peace in the future but, for now, they simply needed to prevent war. And, he needed to get to Mary.

It was well past matins by the time he had been safely able to leave Drum and follow the old stone road northwest that led to the abbey.

William's stomach remained in constant knots every moment that passed and he had not reached Mary. Her wails echoed in his heart. He should have fought James to keep Mary with him at Drum, curse it all. James may be her guardian, but William was her betrothed, and he had let her down and allowed her to be humiliated in front of the entire clan because he had gotten carried away with his feelings for her, the need to love her. And yet, coward that he was, he had made love to her without saying the words he desired to speak, that she deserved to hear.

Even now, the scent of her fresh, clean skin lingered in his mind. Her breasts had been warm and soft in his hands, and his lips had never tasted anything sweeter than their rosy ripe buds. She was more than just intelligence and beauty. She was sensual, honest, loyal, and all the things he ever wanted in a woman. And now, he may have lost her forever.

Urging his horse past the thickly wooded land on either side of the old knobby trail, William gripped the reins so tightly, he felt the leather digging into his flesh. He should be halfway to the abbey by now and wondered if he would even be allowed in, or if James had made certain he would not be allowed near Mary.

The sound of another rider approaching from the north made William pull back, bringing his horse to a halt. It was nearly pitch black and the light of the moon eerily glowed through the wall of clouds in the sky, creating a mystical haze and causing the fresh white snow to almost glow. It was all William had to light his way, but he had navigated in less. "Who approaches?" he asked, placing his hand on the hilt of his sword. Thieves should not be a threat with the snow falling as thick as it was, but Scotland was never short of men looking for trouble.

When the rider slowed beside him, William scowled and popped his knuckles. "Where is she?"

"I didnae drag her away from ye just to tell ye where she is. Mary is safe."

"She isnae safe if she is alone. Her child is due and there is a certain man missing that I dinnae trust." William sighed and pushed his tangled hair away from his face. "James, if ye wish to keep me away from Mary, ye had better kill me now. Death is the only thing that will prevent me from finding her."

Shifting in his saddle, James narrowed his eyes on William, scrutinizing him. "Would ye fight me to the death for her hand?"

Dismounting his horse without hesitation, William placed his hand on his sword and nodded. "I dinnae wish to harm ye. I ken Mary loves ye, and I willnae cause her more grief. But I will fight ye. First to draw blood." He was not frightened by James and though he was confident in his own fighting skills, he was certain James would be well-trained and a formidable foe. He was not afraid of death but dying without seeing Mary once more caused him more pain than the thought of eternal darkness.

James hopped down from his horse and slowly walked toward William, clearly sizing him up and determining his worth as a warrior. William knew his skills on the battlefield. They had been tested too many times. He was not selected to be the king's Marischal and protector during parliament for no reason.

"Would ye die to save her?" James asked, his gaze still narrowed on William.

"Do ye believe ye can kill me?" William asked in reply. "Many men have tried, yet none have succeeded. But, aye. I would die to save her, and if ye keep her away from those she loves, if ye make her birth her bairn alone, ye are sentencing her to a life of misery."

"What if I told ye that she was marrying another man right now?" James shrewdly asked, and William clenched his teeth, his gut twisting.

"That bastard Stephan?" he growled, popping his knuckles. "What have ye done, James?"

The stone façade covering his face crumbled away and William saw a flicker of fear in James' eyes. "How did ye ken I referred to Stephan? He is the man who wrote to me about her condition."

"He wants Mary and always has. He threatened me at the tournament, vowing she would be his. Within hours..." William stopped, horror turning his blood to ice. "Brian was found dead. Then ye arrived and he went missing. It was a diversion."

"What was? What are ye saying, man?" James stepped even closer, this time no longer looking as if he wished to run William through.

"He killed one of my warriors, not a Douglas. Killing Brian made us all turn against one another while he plotted. Did he mention the kirk to ye in the missive?"

Wide-eyed as it all came together in his mind, James nodded slowly but stayed silent.

Cursing under his breath, William watched his frantic breath leave his mouth in visible wisps, disappearing into the wind. "He kenned ye had arrived and would take her away to the kirk. We were all too concerned with finding the murderer to protect Mary from the true threat!" William roared and rubbed his forehead, kicking himself for being a blind fool. "He must have kenned that Brian insulted Marjorie the night before, mayhap overheard it. It was the perfect plan. Is he with Mary right now, James?"

"Nay. She is safe at the kirk. I told the priest not to allow any other men inside until I arrived. William..." James paused and finally took his hand off the hilt of his sword. "I have been a fool. I wanted to protect Mary, to keep her safe and innocent. I am just as angry at myself as I am with ye and Alexander. He isnae here, so I am afraid all my spite has fallen on yer shoulders and clouded my judgment. I trusted a faceless man with dark motivations over the man before me, the man Mary loves."

William took his hand off his hilt, as well, and took a steadying breath, wondering if her brother could possibly be correct about her feelings for him. She never confessed any love for him in his presence. If she loved him and wished to tell him, he would find her and make damned certain she had the opportunity to do so. And, if she still needed time to decide her feelings, William would gladly give it, spending every moment of his life making certain she knew how treasured she was.

"Ye are an elder brother, James. I ken the responsibility ye feel for her. I had to entrust my sister with Drum's laird, and he has proven worthy of her, though we came to blows a time or two. I hope ye can now entrust Mary to me. Allow me to prove I am worthy of her."

"I do believe 'tis I who must prove to be worthy of her now, William," James said so quietly that William almost missed the words. "I treated her most foul, like a wee lass. The truth is, she has become a woman in the years since I have seen her. She speaks her mind freely and had much to say to me before I left the kirk. 'Twas nothing pleasant, but everything I deserved."

Scoffing, William nodded and widened his eyes. "Och, aye. I do ken this about her. She had much to say to me in the beginning, and none of it was easy to hear. Eventually, she learned to tolerate me. But, I'm not the one who carried her off to a kirk. Ye have much more to atone for than I ever did. Ye can start by taking me to her."

James mounted his horse and William heard the torment in the man's voice. "Ye dinnae ken the awful things I said to her. Finding her with ye... I still want to bloody yer nose," he warned.

"And I still want to split yer lip," William shot back. "Ye took Mary from me, humiliated her, sent her to a kirk, and forced Stephan on her!" William said as he climbed back onto his horse, feeling his temper rise once more as the image of Mary being carried away with tears in her eyes haunted him.

"We can pummel each other until we are both bloody another time," James casually replied. "We must get back to Mary. Are ye certain about Stephan?"

"I am certain of nothing more than the facts. Brian is dead, Stephan is missing, Mary is alone, and I will die before I allow him near her." He could not help the accusation in his voice, but James had acted without all the facts, too angry to listen. Glaring at James one last time, William kicked his horse's flanks, taking off down the path at a pace not even the devil himself could keep up with.

William prayed that he was wrong about Stephan, but his instincts were seldom incorrect. Either way, there was no time to waste. He needed to find Mary and fix the damage her brother had caused, then head back to Drum, praying it was still in one piece when he got back.

PACING BACK AND forth in her nearly empty room, Mary chewed on her fingernail and nervously wrung her skirt in her other hand. Every second that passed felt like an eternity within the cold, stone walls. Only one candle adorned her room, its flame flickering in tandem with the draft coming from the ancient halls just beyond her door.

Grabbing the thin wool blanket from the small bed that occupied the corner, Mary wrapped it around her body and shivered. She was not locked away. The prioress had allowed her to roam the kirk that had been built during the reign of King Stephen hundreds of years ago. Though the allure of being within this sacred place was strong, Mary dared not leave her room. Alexander's effigy was not far away, and she found that she lacked the strength to seek it out. Would he ever forgive her for loving another man?

The bell outside rang for lauds and the sudden break in the otherwise silent room caused Mary to jump and gasp. It was nearing dawn and she had no notion when James would return for her, but she prayed he did not hurt the people she loved most. He was not an unfair man, but he was proud and easily angered when he felt the honor of the clan was on the line.

Hands trembling, Mary reached out to unbar the door, the rough wood scraping into her soft flesh. It was heavier than expected and Mary grunted as she moved it aside and slowly pushed the door open. Her soft leather slippers made no noise as she took a step into the dark hall, lit with sparse sconces along the wall. The lingering chill was enough to make her wrap the blanket even tighter around her body. It felt as if the spirits of hundreds of warriors and nobles haunted the very space she walked through.

Gooseflesh ran up her legs and covered her arms. The priory rooms were set in the far back of the cathedral, and the long, stretching hall appeared to go on forever. According to the kind priest who had greeted her, Alexander's effigy was in the transept of the cathedral. Dare she seek him out? A cramp made her womb tense up into a hard knot, and Mary bent over, gritting her teeth through the pain, trying to remember to breathe.

"Alexander, look what ye left me with," Mary whispered into the darkness and wondered if he could hear her. It was now or never. His effigy was somewhere within these walls. Shuffling into the area of the cathedral that made the room appear to be a cross, Mary stopped and looked around at the centuries-old architecture and effigies of lairds, lords, knights, and royals who had been brought to rest throughout the years.

Bile burned in her throat to think of Alexander, the warm, strong man who had held her so lovingly at night, now lying still and cold within the confines of a stone effigy here in this kirk.

"Nay. I cannae do this." Turning away, Mary started to flee, then stopped as something caught her eyes. It was him. His very likeness carved into stone at the far side of the transept. "Alex?" Mary spoke his name, knowing he would not respond. But he was here. She felt him, his comforting presence enveloping her.

Taking a slow step toward him, then another and another, Mary finally was face to face with the likeness of the man whose child now wedged a heel into her ribs. Hesitating, Mary touched the rough, cold stone beneath her fingertips and pulled away. When he had left for battle last summer, never had she expected the next time she laid eyes on him would be like this, staring at his image preserved forever, expertly sculpted for all to see for centuries.

"Oh, Alex." Running her hand down the ridges of armor, she wondered at how accurate it was. Robert must have paid a sculptor very well to honor his brother's image. It was beautiful, yet haunting. Bending over, Mary rested her forehead on his, placing her hands over his and sighed. "I am here, Alex. I am sorry I never came before. I am weak, and I confess this. James forced me to come here to repent for my sins. I wonder if he kenned I needed to repent to ye more than a priest. 'Tis been the most painful time of my life without ye."

Swallowing back her tears, she closed her eyes and took a few steadying breaths. "Ye ken I loved ye more than aught, and I will always hold ye close to my heart. Yer child grows stronger daily. If only ye had lived to ken of him. Alex... I must confess something to ye..."

The tears began to fall in earnest. There was no holding them back. Her throat constricted and her heart felt as if it were being crushed in by a fist. "I... I am to be married to another man. Ye met him once. His name is William Keith and he is Elizabeth's brother if ye can believe that. We always dreamed of getting married to each other, didnae we? But we were destined for other paths and other fates. Oh, Alexander. I havenae even spoken the hardest words of all."

Taking her forehead off his, Mary stared into the still likeness of him. The nose was slightly smaller and the lips a wee bit thinner, but the face she looked at was his own, and it made her insides quake. "I am in love with him, Alexander." The words came rushing out of her so fast, she thought she may lose her breath, but they were said. "I never thought it possible to love another, but he is a verra good man, and he has vowed to raise yer child. Between ye and me, I do believe the bairn is a lad. I just… feel it. He is strong and must have much hair, for the burning in my stomach has been intense and the midwives all say he will be born with as much hair as his father had." Mary giggled at that image in her mind and shook her head.

"I hope ye will forgive me for loving another. Robert vows ye would wish me to move on and find happiness, and I find I do agree. Ye loved me so well, Alex, and I will treasure our times together forever. But, my life continues and I must make room for William and love him just as well as I loved ye. It is only right, and he deserves that. He is good to me. Ye would approve, even if James doesnae," she scowled. "Yer son will be born any day, I believe. 'Tis hard to ken, yet the pains come often and he is a big lad, always kicking my ribs and moving around inside me. I wish ye could have felt him."

Kissing her fingertips, Mary placed them on his sculpted lips and smiled. "Ye are so loved and verra missed. I ken ye can hear me now, Alex. I dinnae ken how to say goodbye to ye. I didnae then, and I cannae now. So, I will simply vow to see ye once again after yer child is born. Ye must meet him, for I ken he will be strong like his father. They sing ballads about ye… do ye ken that? Do ye watch over us and listen while we tell tales of ye? I think ye do. I have felt it. Ye will always be with us, Alexander. Rest well with our Lord. And ken that I think of ye every day."

Fighting back a new round of tears, Mary decided enough was enough. She could stand there all night and talk to Alexander, but to what end? Turning around, Mary meant to run away as fast and as far as she could but, instead, she plowed into a solid object, this one warm and softer than stone. Looking up, Mary gasped and took a step back, feeling Alexander's effigy behind her wobbly knees.

"H-how are ye here?" Fear crawled up her spine, causing her hackles to rise. The candles flickered around the cathedral walls, casting eerie shadows. Surely, he was not as crazed as he appeared when the light hit his face.

"Surprised? Thought ye were alone while ye spoke to yer dead lover?"

Mary flinched and her gut roiled. "Stephan... how did ye get in here? My brother ordered that no man could come looking for me in here."

"Oh, I have my ways." He took a small step closer, and she attempted to step back but instead fell onto Alexander's effigy, hissing when the sharp curves of stone dug into her thighs and backside.

His calm, stonelike demeanor made warning bells sound in her head. How long had he sat there and listened to her private words? His presence was unsettling, and his words even more so.

"Did James send ye here? Ye betrayed me! Now I cannae go back to Drum!" Though her voice quaked, she felt her anger rise along with her tone. She was cornered like a cat and ready to claw her way out if necessary.

"I didnae betray ye! Alexander did when he refused to wed with ye and put that bastard in yer belly! Ye have been blinded by that man, and now William. Ye cannae see the truth before ye." He leaned over, placing his cold hands on her shoulders, their chill seeping through the thin fabric of her under tunic. Shrugging him away, Mary pulled the thin blanket back around her body as tightly as she could to stave him off, but he simply grabbed her once more. Believing herself alone and safe, Mary had not bothered to replace her clothing before wandering the halls, a decision she deeply regretted as Stephan's lecherous gaze had raked over her body before she covered herself.

"What truth, Stephan?" She tried to remain calm, but he refused to directly answer any of her questions. And when he referred to her child as a bastard, the urge to claw his eyes out made her clench her hands into fists.

"That ye were meant to be mine all along. I didnae betray ye,

Mary. I saved ye. Now ye willnae be ruined. And we can finally be together, the way God intended." Stephan looked down at the tops of her breasts that were not covered by the blanket, and licked his lips, making her wish to recoil. God had nothing to do with the gleam of lust in his dark eyes. They were like looking at mirrors of his soul, dark and empty but for his own desires.

Shaking her head, Mary closed her eyes. He was close. Too close. And she was vulnerable, a feeling she had always strived to avoid. There was no avoiding now that she was at his mercy and knew that he had none. His course palms slid down her shoulders and yanked the blanket out of her grasp, making Mary jump and yelp in fear. Throwing the blanket to the ground, Stephan then slid his hands over her breasts, where he cupped them through her under tunic, groaning her name. Swallowing hard, Mary shook.

"Mayhap I shall have ye right here. Right on top of Alexander's grave so he can see the wanton whore ye truly are... I want him to hear ye scream another man's name. Ye allowed William to touch ye. Am I not worthy of the same honor?" As Stephan's voice grew more sinister, Mary's fear grew more intense. He did not care that they were in a kirk, or that Alexander's body was so near. Madman that he was, Stephan was enjoying it all the more.

Stephan pinched her nipples until she yelped and tried to twist away. "Please, Stephan... ye cannae..." she whispered, doing her best to keep a clear head.

"I cannae?" Pushing the fabric down her shoulders, Stephan smiled when her bared breasts became exposed to his eager gaze. "I believe I can. I believe I shall."

Before she could think or react, Stephan grabbed her by both arms and tossed her onto her back, the freezing stone floors of the cathedral seeping through her under tunic and into her flesh. "Stephan!" she cried and grunted when her head hit the floor, pain exploding in her skull. Disoriented, Mary grabbed her head with one hand and tried to fight him off with the other, but she was too weak and dizzy. Blood coated the hand holding her scalp and she sobbed. "Please!"

It was happening so fast and yet seemed to last forever as every detail etched into her mind. Stephan unbuckling his belt and loosening his breeches. His other hand yanking her under tunic up to her thighs. The feel of his clammy, callused palms running up her leg. The pressure she felt when he attempted to spread her legs and defile her with his filth.

"Nay!" She would not allow this. She had no strength, but she still had her voice. Opening her mouth, she screamed as loud as she could, hoping the priests would be preparing for their prayers somewhere within the kirk. Her temples throbbed from the pain in her head, but she continued to wail with all her might.

Smacking her across the face, Stephan scowled and pulled his breeches back up, quickly replacing his belt. She took that moment to cover her breasts again and attempt to break away, primal fear driving her instinct to survive at all cost, even if her cheek throbbed from his blow and her head ached from her fall.

"Why, Mary? Ye make everything difficult!" Feeling herself being lifted into his arms, Mary kicked and screamed some more, praying someone heard her. She had no idea what he was doing or where he was taking her, but she knew for certain that Stephan had plotted this entire event.

Footsteps echoed through the cathedral from the corridor, and Mary yelled. "Help! Stephan Irvine is–"

Stephan released his hold on her and Mary landed hard on her feet, feeling the shock run up her ankles from the impact. When his hand slapped over her mouth to stifle her shouts, Mary bit the flesh of his palm, making him yelp in pain, but he did not release his grip.

Dragging her across the cathedral, Mary had no choice but to move her feet toward the back of the kirk as he led her from behind, one hand across her mouth and the other behind her. Something sharp poked her back and she arched forward as much as possible, wondering if he had pulled a dagger on her.

"Who is here? Mary?" She heard the familiar voice of the priest who had greeted her earlier but dared not to make a sound. If a knife was truly against her back, she would not risk harm befalling her bairn. Stephan pulled her behind one of the towering columns that ran the length of the cathedral, tightening his grasp on her as a group of three priests searched the area, carrying candles on a stick that likely did not allow them to see more than an arm's length past their noses.

When the men rounded a corner and went down a side corridor, Stephan pushed her along once more, continuing in the same direction. When they reached a smaller, less ornate door at the back of the room, Stephan leaned over and hissed in her ear. "I am going to remove my hand. If ye scream, I will kill ye. Do ye understand?" Mary nodded emphatically and pursed her lips when he removed his hand.

Pulling a long metal key out of a satchel tied to his belt, Stephan unlocked the door, cursing when the ancient hinges groaned. How did Stephan have a key for this door? She would not ask, but the foulest thoughts ran through her mind. Was he capable of murdering a priest? Is that how he gained entry to the kirk? Stephan pushed her through the door and shut it behind him, yanking her by the arm and leading her down a side path through what would likely be a beautiful garden by spring, but was currently covered in leafless shrubs and ankle-deep in fresh snow.

The wind blew Mary's red hair across her face, and she stumbled on a loose rock beneath her feet. "Where are ye taking me?" she finally asked now that they were alone outside. "'Tis c-cold out here." Teeth chattering, Mary did her best to keep up with his long strides. "Stephan... I cannae keep up! The bairn..."

Pulling her into a thickly wooded cove behind the kirk, Stephan pressed her up against a tree and covered her mouth, flashing a blade before her eyes. "I care not for yer bastard!" He growled through clenched teeth, and Mary felt bile burn her throat as she nearly vomited. He would kill her child if she did not get away.

When he began to pull her along once more, Mary saw a cart tucked between the trees in the distance. It was the same one James had delivered her in, and she tried to pull away even when his grip on her wrist threatened to break her bones. "Where are ye taking me, Stephan? James will be back for me. He even left the cart. He will be here soon!"

Snickering at her when they approached the cart, Stephan waved the blade in her face. "Get in." Doing as he commanded, Mary stepped into the cart and pressed as far into the back as she could to avoid his weapon. Stephan climbed in after her, thankfully tucking his dagger back into his boot. She sighed with relief but knew her troubles were far from over. She was alone in a cart with the crazed man who had attempted to force himself on her just moments ago, and she was not certain what he was capable of.

"James isnae coming back for quite some time. There is a dead body at Drum and a murderer they shallnae find. He will be quite occupied with the war that shall wage soon enough when they discover the Irvine plaid soaked in Brian's blood." A salacious grin slid across his face and Mary gasped. He had killed Brian? Stephan was attempting to start a war between the Keiths and Irvines, destroying the hard-earned yet fragile peace they had achieved through the union of Robert and Elizabeth not long ago.

If the Keiths believed an Irvine killed one of their best warriors, peace would be forgotten, and another bloody battle between the two clans would rage. William would be in danger. It was all starting to come together, and yet so much did not make sense. She needed to keep him talking. The look of need in his eyes made her skin crawl.

"Ye killed an innocent man and endangered yer own kin just to start a war? For what purpose? What could possibly be worth such a betrayal?" He was naught more than a landless knight. He had no money, nor power to gain by the deaths of any laird.

"Ye are, Mary. Ye are worth it all. To have ye…" Stephan took a step closer. "To own ye…" Another step brought him face to face with her, and she pressed herself against the rough wooden back of the cart, both her head and lip still throbbing. "To feel ye…" His hands reached out to grab her breasts again, and she slapped them away, disgusted by him.

"Dinnae touch me! Ye shall never own me!" She spat in his face, but he only smiled wider, making her cringe in fear. His eyes were wild and darker than the night as he took her by the shoulders.

"I can, and I will. Nobody is here to hear ye scream now, Mary. And once I have had ye, I shall take ye back to Douglas lands and ye will be my wife."

Bewilderment and horror flooded her. She attempted to break free, but his grip only grew stronger. "Douglas lands?"

"Ye underestimate me." Making a tsking sound, Stephan shook his head. "Ye think that because I grew sickly and have been marred by the scars of my illness, that I am a fool? I ken ye loved me then. I ken ye would have been my wife if I hadnae been ill and Alexander hadnae stolen ye away while I lay half-dead in my bed!" he shouted, and she jumped from the sudden change in his voice.

"I offered for yer hand, Mary, and ye rejected me! Ye chose William over me. I was in the hall when yer brother broke down yer door, only nobody ever pays attention to sickly, pock-faced Stephan Irvine! But the Black Douglas did! He sees me. He understands what drives a man. We made an agreement, and I wrote to yer brother. Once the Hamiltons arrived, they would turn against the Irvines. Then, the Keiths would turn against them when they discovered an Irvine killed Brian. The Black Douglases would turn when they were accused of the murder. And when it was all over, the Irvines would pay in blood, and William would die for daring to take what is mine. I will make ye my wife, and we shall live safely on their lands. After all, I am Douglas."

His last words made her brows lower in confusion, and Stephan sighed with contempt. "Ye never cared to ask about me, did ye? Ye only ever spoke of yer Hamilton kin, but ye never cared to ask about mine. My father was cast out, accused of a crime he didnae commit. My Uncle Archibald was involved in the plot to kill the king's eldest son, placing the current regent closer to the throne. Then, he had the other son captured and sent to England where he still resides today… our verra own King James," Stephan said with contempt.

"Those men were Archibald's brothers by marriage, but gaining power means everything to a Black Douglas. Now, thanks to his help, he has the backing of the regent and can achieve anything. But first, he needed to place the blame elsewhere and his own brother, my father, was too weak to defend himself when the fingers pointed to him and cast him out," Stephan sneered and appeared disgusted by the thought of his own father.

"The Irvines took us in out of pity, kenning he was innocent, but they never truly cared about me. Nobody did… until now. My uncle sees my potential. He told me if I helped him weaken the clans, making his eventual takeover easier, he would offer me a place once more amongst the Black Douglas Clan, where I always belonged. Marjorie is my cousin!" He laughed as if he had made a fine jest, and Mary knew then that there was nothing left of the Stephan she had once known as a child. His illness must have rotten his soul. "I only fought in that tournament to make certain I wasnae nearby when the body was found."

Mary shook her head, the pounding in her skull nearly blinding her as she tried to absorb all he confessed to. The hatred in his soul felt like a living, breathing entity surrounding them within the confines of the cart. Mary listened in horror, never having known Stephan was truly so demented by jealousy. He had gone to great lengths to hurt innocent people, just to have her. A wave of sickness choked her just as a cramp gripped her belly. What if succumbing to Stephan was the only chance she had to survive this, to save her child? Nothing was more important to her than keeping him safe and she would sacrifice everything to do so. She dared to ask, desperate to know how to proceed. "What of my bairn, Stephan? Ye had vowed to raise him as yer own... he will be here soon enough."

"Do ye truly believe I would raise the child of the man who took ye from me? A constant reminder of all yer betrayals? Once the bairn is born, its body can be buried in the snow and eaten by the wolves for all I care, much like the priest I had to kill to get the key to the kirk."

How could he speak of killing a bairn and a priest with so little emotion? Tears streamed down from Mary's eyes and she clutched her abdomen, petrifying terror causing her to tremble. "Ye are sick in the head, Stephan. A madman... ye are full of the devil, ye are..." She would die in this cart. He would slit her throat if she never agreed to marry him, and there was no way to escape. Either way, her child would die. Shaking all over, Mary slid down the side of the cart and tucked herself into a ball, having no more energy or ideas. She was truly stuck with a demon in this cart, and her head felt ready to explode from the pain her wound caused.

Kneeling in front of her, Stephan gently tucked her hair behind her ear and swiped a tear off her chin, touching it to his tongue and closing his eyes. Mary cringed at the odd delight he took in tasting her tears and tried to turn away, but he gripped her chin with his fingers and forced her to look at him. "I saw William with his hands all over what belongs to me. I heard ye claim to be betrothed to him, heard James say he was bringing ye to Alexander. I followed behind. Nobody sees me. Ye dinnae see me." Stephan narrowed his eyes on Mary, and the smile slid from his face. Holding her breath, she awaited the ensuing attack. "Ye see me now, dinnae ye, Mary, my love? And now 'tis time to make ye mine."

Grabbing her legs, Stephan pulled them out from beneath her, forcing her onto her back. "Nay! She kicked with all her strength, but she had little left. Her mind was warning her to give in to him, to allow him to believe she had succumbed so she could strike when he was not prepared. If his guard was down, she could run. Yet, her body rejected his touch. His very nearness made her recoil with disgust.

He pinned down her legs and she knew it was over. She would not win this battle, and James would wage his own battle on the innocent Irvines. He would not arrive before she was already gone, and William would be lost to her forever.

"Please… dinnae hurt my bairn, Stephan. I will marry ye. Just… dinnae hurt my bairn." Her body went limp as all the fight left her. If she had a chance of saving her child, this was it. Fighting him had done her no good and would only lead to disaster. She had already lost everyone she had ever loved. Losing her child was not a reality she would accept. Closing her eyes, she felt the darkness clawing at her, determined to pull her under.

"Get yer hands off of my sister!" The cover of the cart was slashed through with the tip of a sword and Mary screamed, forcing her eyes open and scrambling to the back of the cart the moment Stephan loosened his grip on her legs.

Was she bleeding so profusely from the head that she was imagining her brother? When his face appeared, her vision wavered, and she felt as if she would be sick. "James?"

He did not respond, but as he reached into the cart and dragged Stephan out by his tunic, Mary gripped her heart, knowing she was not hallucinating.

"Mary!" The familiar voice of the man she loved floated to her ears and, once again, she questioned her sanity. But when he jumped into the back of the cart and wrapped her in his strong embrace, the familiar scent of his skin and feel of his flesh told her she was not imagining his presence.

"Will?" Her voice was weak and though she tried to keep her head upright, it lulled to the side, resting on his shoulder.

"Ye're bleeding!" Panic shook his voice, but she simply made a sound of agreement and closed her eyes, finally safe in his arms and giving in to the sleep that beckoned her.

CHAPTER TEN

ARRIVING AT THE kirk, William immediately jumped off his horse, a bone-deep wave of dread rolling through him like a wave pulling him under. The entrance was open and several priests held candles, scanning the area for something... or someone.

James was right behind him, obviously having the same ominous thoughts. "Where is my sister?"

One priest slowly walked over to them with worry creasing his elderly face, wringing his hands together. "We are looking for her, Sir James. She... is gone."

"What do ye mean? She wouldnae have left, not in her condition!" William looked at James and scowled. "This is yer doing! Ye forced her to come here!"

Scanning the area, James shook his head. "Aye. 'Tis my fault. I was cruel and unrelenting. I threatened to take her child away if she wouldnae marry Stephan."

"Ye... ye arenae deserving of her love! Ye would threaten such a thing?" Anger welled up inside William, a red haze clouding his vision. Shoving James with all his strength, he watched as her brother stumbled back, then charged at him, knocking William to the ground.

"I wouldnae have had to do it if ye could have kept yer hands off my sister, ye bastard!" James swung his right fist, connecting with William's gut.

"We are betrothed!" William shot back, not willing to allow the pain in his stomach to stop him from giving James what he deserved. Rolling over, he brought James with him, landing on top, planting his fist into the man's jaw. "I love yer sister and would never dishonor her as ye have! I would never put her in danger as ye have!" Pulling his arm back, he prepared to connect with James' face once more, before he heard the priest release a deafening whistle, making both men instantly stop and look up at the man.

"Sir James, we are afraid for her life. We dinnae believe she ran away. We heard a scream from the cathedral, but when we searched the area, all we found was the open back door to the gardens and a sheet on the ground near an effigy. When we sought out the priest with that key, he wasnae to be found."

"What are ye saying?" William groused as he got off the snow-covered ground, putting a hand out for James. Her brother scowled at him and narrowed his eyes in warning, but he took the peace offering and stood beside William.

"Why would she scream from the cathedral area? Did she not have a private chamber?" James asked with accusation in his voice. "Did the priest do something to her?"

"Nay! Father Benedict wouldnae hurt her, I vow. We believe she was visiting the effigy of a man she had asked about, Sir Alexander Irvine. We told her it was in the transept, which is where the scream seemed to originate. But, she wasnae to be found."

William's gut churned and not from the blow her brother had given him. She still loved Alexander. She had been visiting him and likely pining for the man she loved and lost, whispering sweet sentiments to his likeness. She did not love him, and he had been a fool to ever believe she would. Her love for Alexander was too great, her loss too fresh. She would marry him, aye, but for no other reason than protection and security for her child. Those reasons had been satisfactory to him only days ago, but now he wanted more from Mary. He wanted her to look at him the way she looked when she spoke Alexander's name. He wanted her to whisper words of love to him in the dark. He wanted her to carry his child.

William was jealous of a dead man. The realization nearly blinded him. They had shared their bodies, created a connection he had never known with any woman. He had meant everything he said to her hours before. Mary was the most beautiful woman he had ever known and though he would make her his wife and raise her child, loving them both endlessly, she would silently love another man. The thought made his stomach go sour.

An older woman wearing the clothing of a nun ran out of the kirk shaking her head and wringing her hands with worry. "We cannae find her, Father Benjamin. I vow the last I saw of her was when I showed her to her room."

"Have the grounds been searched?" James asked, a mixture of anger and fear threading his voice.

"Of course, they have!" the priests replied with exasperation. The kirk surely was not used to so much chaos penetrating its peaceful existence.

Stepping closer to James, William rubbed his beard and narrowed his eyes. "'Tis Stephan. I ken it. He killed the missing priest, stole his key, and took Mary," he whispered. Turning to the priest, William asked, "Was there anyone else in the kirk? Any visitors?"

"I demanded nobody else be allowed to enter," James warned.

"Ye demanded that, aye, Son, but 'tis not yer place to tell us our business. If a man comes to seek sanctuary, we willnae turn him away. That isnae God's will. This is His house, not yers. As it happens, no man, except for ye, has arrived here since Mary."

The nun tittered beside the priest and made the sign of the cross. "There was a man, Father. The one who arrived before Mary…"

"What did he look like?" William shouted at the nun and she jumped. He had not meant to frighten her, but his nerves were causing him to shake and lose control of himself.

"He was dark," she whispered ominously, looking around as if fearing the very devil himself was lurking in the shadows. "Not only in his features but in his soul. I felt it. He came asking for sanctuary. We cannae turn away any man, ye ken. His room was in another building and I didnae believe Mary was in danger."

"He took her!" William demanded. "Stephan took her!"

"The cart!" James hollered. "I left the cart in the woods so I could transport her back! Did ye see a cart?" he asked the priests.

"Nay, we saw no cart, Sir James."

Growling and clenching his fists, James took off at a run toward the back of the kirk, and William followed, his heart in his throat as he thought about that madman having Mary in his control. Sharp, barren twigs covered in ice lashed at his arms and face as he maneuvered through the thickly wooded landscape, but nothing was going to stop William from finding Mary. Dread and doubt crept into his mind like poison. What if she was not found or worse, they found her and she was dead? Nay. He willed those thoughts out of his head. They did him no good and he did not suspect that Stephan would go through all this trouble just to kill her.

Coming to a sudden halt, James turned and put his finger to his lips, pointing with his other hand. "The cart is still there."

The ground was covered in snow, the pure white reflecting off the rays of the early morning sun just creeping over the horizon. Squinting into the blinding terrain, he saw the cart in the distance and nodded to James.

Taking careful step by careful step, the hackles on the back of his neck rose when he saw the cart shake and heard Stephan's muffled voice, followed by a thud.

The snow crunched beneath their boots, but William trudged

forward, determined to get to her and kill Stephan if he had harmed Mary.

"Please… dinnae hurt my bairn, Stephan. I will marry ye. Just… dinnae hurt my bairn." Her words were full of desperation as they drifted to his ears, and numbing fear attacked his every sense. Apparently, James heard her plea as well, taking off at a run that matched William's. His feet moved faster than they ever had in his life, as did his heart.

Drawing his sword, James slashed through the cloth covering the cart, shouting at Stephan to get off his sister. Just as William was preparing to enter the cart and slit Stephan's throat for daring to harm Mary, James reached inside and ripped the man out by his tunic. When he fell to the ground with a thud and a grunt, William wished to end the man's life immediately, but he knew James could handle it alone, and he needed to make sure Mary was not harmed.

Hopping into the cart, he saw her and his stomach dropped. Lying on her back, Mary's dress was bunched around her knees as she held her head and kept her eyes closed. Her face looked too serene for a woman in peril, and warning bells rang in his spinning mind.

"Mary!" William lifted her into his arms, wrapping her in his embrace. When her head lulled to the side and she whispered his name and opened her eyes, he placed a hand under her head to support it and felt a warm stickiness coating his palm. "Ye're bleeding!"

Making a small sound, Mary closed her eyes once more and went completely limp. "Mary? Mary!" Gently shaking her, William could not get her to respond. Putting his cheek up to her mouth, he felt her warm breath and knew she was alive. But, she was injured, and fear for her and the child gripped him like a vise.

The sound of struggling outside the cart pulled his attention away for a moment. He wanted to help James but feared for Mary if he left her alone. Her wound needed to be bandaged. Sticking his head out of the cart opening, he saw James pinning Stephan face down in the snow, his knee planted into the man's back as he held his arms behind him. "Is Mary all right?" James shouted when he looked up at William. All William could do was shake his head and turn his attention back to her. Tearing off a piece of his plaid, William tied it around her head to put pressure on her wound.

"Mary... I am so sorry, love." She murmured something in response, and relief flooded him. She was conscious. "We will get ye away from here, I vow. Ye are safe now." With her eyes still shut, Mary moved her weak hand to touch his face, stroking his beard before dropping her arm to her side.

The cart rocked and dipped in the back as James stepped in, looking at him and Mary with a creased brow. "I cannae kill the bastard. He is unarmed," James growled. "I tied up his arms with my plaid, but we need to get back to Drum and let Robert deal with him. Mary? Sister... I am so verra sorry. I failed ye."

Moving her head, Mary winced. "Dagger... boot..."

Dropping his brow, William stroked her cheek. "I think she is saying Stephan has a dagger in his boot. The fact that she kens that is disturbing."

"Nay, I checked his boots. He must have dropped it. He has no weapons and is now tied to a tree."

"Leave him there to rot!" William groused through his clenched teeth. "I ken he killed Brian."

"Then he will pay for his deeds. He is Robert's responsibility. I willnae kill an unarmed man, Will."

A piercing scream shook the cart from within, and William took Mary in his arms once more as she writhed, gripping her belly. "William!"

"Everything is all right, love," he soothed, but she shook her head and gritted her teeth. He knew she was having her pains once more, and he took her hand in his. She bore down with a crushing strength that shocked him.

When the pain passed, Mary went limp once more and closed her eyes. "She is nearing her time," James said with a frown.

"I ken it. She should be at Drum, not stuffed into a cart with a bleeding head wound," he shot back and scowled at her brother. "That man out there..." William pointed outside the cart. "He is the man ye would prefer Mary to wed, aye?"

James ignored his words and looked at his sister. "Mary... I am a cursed fool. I dinnae deserve ye."

"We will get ye back to Drum right away and have Elizabeth and Matilda tend to ye. All will be well," William assured, stroking her arms and wrapping the rest of his torn plaid around her body. Freezing air seeped into the cart, and her shaking limbs concerned him.

"'Tis too late!" she cried and sat up into a ball, screaming once more and clenching her teeth against the pain. "The bairn comes!" Tears ran down her cheeks and sweat dotted her brow.

"Now?" James asked, looking around at the barren trees surrounding them, nothing but the kirk around for miles.

"Now!" she roared. Collapsing back into the hay, Mary panted and whimpered like an injured animal.

"Ye willnae birth our child in the back of a cursed cart," William assured her and scooped her up into his arms. "James, open the back. We must get her inside the kirk."

James stared at his sister with disbelief, turning as white as the snow that covered the earth. "James! Now!" William roared, and James blinked his eyes, snapping out of whatever spell he had temporarily been under. Hopping out of the cart, James lifted the latch and lowered the back, allowing William to safely climb down, cradling Mary in his arms.

"Run ahead to the kirk. Tell the prioress that Mary is in labor. They will ken what to do."

Nodding his understanding but remaining silent for the first time since William had met the man, James took off at a run toward the kirk entrance.

"Ye cannae leave me out here!" Stephan shouted from the tree he was tied to. "I will die out here!"

Groaning, Mary shifted in his arms and rested her head against his shoulder. The torn plaid wrapped around her head was a reminder of all that Stephan was truly capable of and William scowled at the man.

"Mayhap ye should have thought of that before ye attacked an innocent woman carrying a child!" William spat at Stephan's feet and scowled. "I would leave ye here to rot for what ye have done, but I willnae deny Robert the pleasure of deciding yer fate. Tell me one thing. Did ye kill my warrior?"

Stephan's face slowly morphed before his eyes. He went from a look of distress to one of mirth blended with pride. "It wasnae personal, ye ken. He was a convenient sacrifice in the games of war."

"War?" William wished to know more, but Mary writhed in his arms and cried out in torment. "James will be back to take ye to Drum, and ye shall suffer!" William shouted as he turned and ran toward the kirk.

Stephan was a foul, loathsome excuse for a man and though William had no idea what he meant about war, the words set unease into his bones and he knew danger was brewing back at Drum.

When he reached the entrance, the doors were wide open as the prioress awaited them and signaled William to follow, leading him down a corridor that brought them to a separate wing of the kirk. Unlocking a door with a heavy metal key, the prioress swung the door open, its rusted hinges squeaking in protest.

"Bring her in here, quickly now." As other nuns stood by awaiting their orders, the prioress continued to guide William while shouting commands to bring fresh linens and warm water to the room. She was certainly not the meek and tittering nun he had witnessed upon his arrival, and it gave him the much-needed hope that Mary would receive the help she required.

"My name is Mother Frances. I am also a midwife. Mary is in good care. Ye must place her on this bed and go."

William did as he was told and gently placed Mary down onto a clean mattress covered in fresh white linen sheets, but he refused to leave her side. "I willnae leave." Mary fluttered her eyes and attempted to smile at him, searching for his hand with hers. Another pain wracked her body and she wailed, more tears running down her cheeks.

"I am the father and I willnae leave her."

The nun pushed him aside and placed a cushion beneath Mary's wrapped head. "I dinnae care if ye are the father of the bairn or father of this kirk! The birthing room is no place for a man!"

"Will..." Mary squeezed his hand. "I will be... all right."

"I dinnae wish to leave ye, Mary." Kissing her forehead, he felt her sweat-slicked skin and looked at her bandaged head. "I fear for ye."

"Stephan... is a... Douglas," she whispered, squeezing her eyes shut as if every word cost her dearly. The wound on her head must have pained her greatly, she seemed determined to speak. "Drum. War... tell James."

Another roar of pain tore through Mary and she bellowed in agony. Sister Frances ran over to her with a wet linen, placing it on her forehead, then moved to the foot of the bed. "I must examine the lady. Ye must leave."

Finally accepting that he was not welcome in the birthing chamber, William pushed away his disappointment and gave Mary's hand one last squeeze. "I will leave this chamber, but I willnae leave the kirk. I will relay yer warning to James and send him to Drum with Stephan." Releasing her hand, William slowly walked toward the door, reluctant to leave her side. He feared for her life, and for the child. He knew childbirth was a dangerous business, and many women and children did not survive it. Mary would... she had to. He could not live without her. But she was the very strongest woman he had ever known and he prayed all would be well.

Before he stepped foot out of the door, William turned around and looked at Mary. If there was ever a time to tell her how he truly felt about her, it was now. He was not even certain she would remember his words, but they had to be said. "I love ye with my whole heart, Mary. I willnae leave this kirk until ye are leaving with me, I vow."

Stepping out of the chamber and into the hall, William quietly shut the door behind him and strode down the long, narrow hall, every footstep echoing around him. The ancient stone walls did nothing to keep the chill of winter at bay, but he never minded the cold over-much. Locating the kirk's entrance, he stepped into the snow, looking around for any sign of James.

He was not in front of the kirk, so William walked around to the back near the garden, seeking out the area in the woods where the cart had been parked. Stephan was no longer tied to the tree, but the cart was still there. Pulling out his sword, William stared at the cart, taking slow steps toward it. "James?"

When his companion did not reply, William froze, searching his surroundings for any sign of foul play. He saw no tracks nor footprints. The snow had successfully covered any sign of movement in the area and William cursed beneath his breath. The back of the cart was still down and he could see nothing but a pile of hay inside.

"Stephan, if ye are hiding in here, come out now before I run ye through." Waiting a moment, he heard no sounds of movement. "Ye have been warned." The man did not deserve a warning at all. If it was not for William's cursed honor as a knight, he would have killed Stephan already, armed or not.

Thrusting his sword into the hay, he met with no resistance. Where was the bloody bastard? And where was James? Turning around, nothing but leafless trees and their gnarly branches were to be seen. Mayhap James had already left for Drum, taking Stephan with him on his horse. Nothing seemed to make sense, but as he scoured the surrounding area, he saw nothing unusual. Checking the stables, his own horse remained comfortably within, chewing on hay and appearing at ease, yet James' horse was missing. William muttered a curse under his breath. James left before William had had a chance to relay Mary's message of warning, but there was naught William could do. He needed to stay here and take care of Mary, relying on James to prove himself worthy of this task.

Walking back into the kirk and sheathing his sword, William paced in circles, worrisome scenarios replaying in his mind: the chance of harm coming to Mary or the child. War at Drum. Elizabeth's safety. William was a man of action and did not like feeling helpless. It reminded him of watching his mother slowly die from a wasting sickness when he was a lad. His father had wailed for days when she died, and William was unable to stop her death or calm his father. At least he had been able to comfort his sister, which was more than he could currently do for Mary, whose screams of turmoil could be heard echoing through the halls.

Starting to run in her direction, William stopped himself and pulled at his hair, reminding himself that he was not allowed near her, yet frustrated by his inability to help James or Mary or Drum.

Turning back toward the chapel, William grumbled under his breath, restlessness and anxiety eating away at him. Taking a deep breath, he walked further into the cathedral, looking at the lit sconces, their fires dancing with the breeze permeating the ancient building and casting ominous shadows across the walls.

A few effigies rested in the transept of the cathedral and William stopped in his tracks. The spirits of fallen soldiers were surely adding to the somber feelings looming in the air, chilling him to the bone. One effigy caught his eye, not because of the intricately carved armor, but because the features etched in stone looked familiar. Reginald and Robert both bore a strong resemblance to one another in the bone structure of their faces, and the man carved in stone just a few feet away looked very much the same. William had, of course, met the living, breathing man, had even called him brother while he lived. Alexander had been married to Elizabeth for so short a time, and though his love for Mary had been no secret to those who knew him, Alexander had treated Elizabeth well, and William had respected him as a man, warrior, laird, and brother-by-marriage.

Walking slowly toward the effigy, William wondered how he could feel so much envy for the man who lay beneath the stone slab. He was gone, and yet he was everywhere. He would never hold Mary in his arms again, and yet he would always hold her heart. William could not compete with this man, for even in death, Alexander was more beloved than William could ever be. His stomach tightened into a knot as he stood before it and looked down at the man, inspecting his armor and the well-made likeness. Even in cold, hard stone, he was a handsome man. His nameplate glittered in the light cast by the fire, and William kneeled beside him, swallowing the lump in his throat.

"Alexander." His voice was husky with emotion and gooseflesh spread over his body when he spoke the man's name. The woman William loved was birthing this man's child down the corridor, her cries carrying through the ancient walls. It felt like dark tidings, and a chill ran up his spine. "I didnae ever expect to be here, to be fool enough to attempt to speak with ye. And yet, for some reason, I ken ye can hear me. Can ye hear her? She is birthing yer child, Alex."

Silence consumed the cathedral. He was alone, yet he was not. "I love her, Alex. I tried not to. Do ye remember when I first arrived at Drum with my sister? Who kenned then that ye would die at Harlaw, Elizabeth would marry yer brother, and Mary would marry yer brother-by-marriage?" William grunted when he said that out loud. It seemed like the most unusual situation, even to his own ears.

"Ye were a good man. A brave man. Ye died fighting for yer people. Mary has missed ye greatly. I admit that I envy ye, as foolish as that sounds while ye lay here beneath a cold slab of rock. She loves ye in a way that she will never love me. But, I will love her eternally, just the same. I will care for her and yer child just as well as ye would have, I vow. I dinnae ken why I am speaking to ye now, except to ease yer soul... and mayhap my own. If ye are here, please watch over Mary and the bairn. Please. I fear they willnae survive the birthing, and I have never been more afraid in my entire life. I have faced the fiercest enemies on the battlefield and, yet, this is what frightens me most. A woman and a child," William said wryly.

Startled by heavy footsteps behind him, William stiffened his back and spun on his heels, hand on his hilt. When he saw James swiftly striding toward him with snow in his hair and ruddy cheeks, he was confused, yet relieved that it was a living man and not a dead one. Mayhap speaking to spirits was messing with his mind and making William believe in more than he should.

"What are ye doing here, James? I thought ye were headed back to Drum?"

James appeared winded but shook the snow off his head and growled. "Where is Mary?"

"She is giving birth in the priory and is being attended by a nun who willnae allow me near her," he grumbled.

"Have ye seen Stephan? I am worried about my sister's safety." James bent over to catch his breath, and William stepped closer, eyes growing wide with concern.

"What? Nay. He wasnae at the tree when I went back. I thought ye left with him."

James blew out a strong breath and ran his fingers through his long, tangled hair. "The moment we left him to bring Mary to the kirk, the bastard escaped! He was tied to that tree verra well. I took my horse out to find him, but he had disappeared. I found tracks heading south, but they disappeared into the woods, away from the kirk."

William ground his teeth and clenched his fists. That madman was on the loose and Mary was vulnerable once again. "Mary mentioned his dagger. He must have hidden it, then used it to cut himself free and fled."

"Aye. The tracks lead toward the old road out of Aberdeen. I dinnae believe he is anywhere near here."

"Toward Douglas lands..." William muttered, rubbing his rough beard with his hand, wishing he had killed Stephan while he had the chance.

Dropping his eyebrows, James looked at William. "Why would the arse head toward Douglas lands?"

"I tried to tell ye, but ye were gone. Mary couldnae speak much but warned that Stephan is a Douglas. It was all a setup. He killed my Keith warrior to turn us against the Douglases, which turned the Irvines on them, as well. He wrote ye that missive, turning the Hamiltons against the Irvines. He said something about a war when he was tied up. He has set us against one another and I fear for my sister back at Drum."

"Aye, I ken she is with child, as well," James said matter-of-factly, and William felt as if he would fall over on his arse with shock.

"Lizzie is having a bairn?"

"Ye didnae ken it? Mary told me on the way here."

"Nay, I didnae ken!" he shot back, feeling pulled between the urge to protect both the women he loved most in this world. He could not be by Mary's side, but he could not go to Elizabeth. "James, ride like the devil to Drum. Tell them that Mary is safe at the kirk having her child, and I am with her. Call the Hamiltons off the Irvines. There is no need for yer clans to be enemies. I will marry yer sister, and we shall all have peace. Whatever ye do, tell Robert about Stephan killing Brian. My men will wish to slaughter Irvines if they find out and I'm not there to command them, but I need ye to tell them my orders. Do ye understand? 'Tis up to ye, James."

"I understand. I already failed Mary. I shallnae fail ye."

"She loves ye, James. But the Irvines are her kin, as well. She will

148

forgive ye. Just stop this madness."

Nodding, James placed a hand on William's shoulder. "I was wrong about ye. I couldnae ask for a better man for my sister. Tell her I love her and that, if the child is a lad, he had better share my name."

William scoffed. "Like hell, he will."

Sending him a wry smirk, James turned and fled the cathedral, leaving William alone with naught but his spinning thoughts, Mary's echoing screams, and the spirit of her dead lover.

CHAPTER ELEVEN

S HE WOULD NOT survive this. The pain exploding in her head with
every scream rivaled the pain tearing through her abdomen with
every contraction. The prioress attempted to soothe her, but nothing
she said could be heard through the ringing in her ears.

The minutes turned to hours, and Mary had no idea how long she
had been in this room attempting to birth Alexander's bairn, but it felt
like an eternity of endless pain shooting through every part of her.
How did some women do this ten times in one lifetime? She would
never have another child. William could go to the devil. He had said
he loved her just before leaving the room and though her heart soared
when she heard those sweet words, the rest of her had been in agony
ever since.

Gritting her teeth, Mary clenched her fists into the linen of her
bunched under tunic, her legs pushed up into her abdomen. "Push, my
lady!"

She had no choice but to obey. Her body was forcing her to
whether she wished to or not. There was no control to be had as this
child was expelled from her womb one excruciating push at a time.

"I cannae…" she sighed, squeezing her eyes closed.

"Ye must, lass," the prioress said calmly, rubbing a horrid smelling herbal balm into her calves as if that were the solution to all her current troubles. Her calves may very well be the one area of her body that did not feel as if they were being torn to shreds.

"I... am tired. I want William."

"He is just outside awaiting ye." Another cramp came on strong, squeezing like a vise. Mary cried out and wished she would just die and be done with the pain. Pushing as hard as she could, her head pulsed against the linens secured around her wound. Curse Stephan. Curse William, and Alexander, as well. Curse James and Robert and even Reginald simply for being men who did not need to ever birth a human!

"This is all their fault!" she cried.

The prioress gave her a grunt of agreement. "The bible blames Eve, but I ken better than that. I may be a nun, but I can see who is really to blame. 'Tis why I took the veil," she said calmly, rubbing Mary's leg. "I wish I could give ye something for the pain in yer head, lass, but I cannae risk harming the bairn."

Opening her eyes, Mary looked at the prioress and suddenly envied her decision to remain chaste as another wave of excruciating agony tore through her. "Damn ye, Alex!" she cried.

"*Mary...*" a voice drifted to her ears like a caress and she gasped at the familiarity of it. She looked around but did not see anyone aside from the nun between her legs.

"He is crowning, Mary! He is almost here!" the woman said with relief. "One more push, lass, and ye shall be a mother!"

"*Mary...*"

"Alexander?" she whimpered, looking around the room. Her head wound was causing her to go mad, hearing a voice from a man she was certain was not here. "It cannae be."

A candle in the corner of the room rapidly flickered then went out, catching her attention as the smoke billowed up to the ceiling. A draft washed over her flesh, giving her gooseflesh all over her arms and legs, yet the door remained locked and there were no windows. Chills crept up her spine as she felt another pain forcing her to push. "I am dying!" she howled. "I willnae survive this!"

A shadow appeared in the corner of the room where the candle had gone out, casting a long shadow over the wall. She saw him. He was as faint as the very smoke filling the room, but he was there, standing tall and flashing the mischievous grin that had made her once fall in love with him. "Alex..."

The figure nodded, staring at her though he seemed to be fading. *"'Tis not yer time, lass. Ye have a long life to live, yet. William will take care of ye and our son. I am sorry it cannae be me, but I want ye happy, Mary. I shall always love ye... be free of me."* Mary blinked back the tears that ran down her face, and when she opened her eyes, he was gone and the candle was lit once more.

"Alexander!" Crying out, Mary heaved as hard as she could, using all the residual strength she did not know she even had, feeling her child being ripped from her body, hearing the cry of new life entering the room.

"'Tis a lad!" the nun whispered reverently. "A stout lad, at that. Just like his father, aye?"

Mary looked at the corner once more and felt her chest tighten with a slurry of emotions. The candle's flame burned brightly once more, and the shadow was gone. "Aye, just like his father." Wiping away her torrent of tears, Mary watched the nun wipe her son clean and wrap him in a blanket before handing him over to her.

Holding her child for the first time, Mary smelled his head, full of thick blond hair the same color as his father's. Her heart was overflowing with love. The most perfect human lay within her arms, and she would die a million times over to keep him safe. All the pain endured to bring him into this world was worth every moment, and she now understood why women had ten children... mayhap not ten, but at least four, she decided.

"Greetings, wee lad. Welcome to the world. I am yer mama." He whimpered and moved his lips, pushing against her chest.

"He is hungry!" Moving forward, the prioress helped Mary pull her under tunic down, allowing her breast to be freed, her son immediately latching on to the nipple like a starved kitten.

"But, I dinnae have any milk yet," she whispered, suddenly worried that her child would starve.

"Och, of course, ye do. See there?" Looking down, Mary noticed her other breast was already leaking as a large wet spot formed on the fabric covering the nipple. "God is a wonderful creator, isnae he?" The prioress smiled and patted Mary's arm. "All ye need to provide him with is nourishment and love, lass. The rest will be provided for ye. I will go get William now. He must be going half-mad." The nun shuffled out of the room, and Mary smiled down at her new son as he instinctively fed from her body. It truly was a miracle. He was perfect.

When he opened his eyes for the first time, looking up at her while he nursed, she saw his hazel eyes and grinned. It was too early to tell, but it appeared he would be the perfect combination of her and his father.

The door opened once more and William immediately strode in, coming to her side with a hesitant smile. "Mary." Standing beside her, he touched her son's wee head and chuckled. "He is a braw laddie, isnae he? He is perfect," William whispered and looked her in the eyes, his features softening. "Are ye all right? I have been worried over ye. I was afraid I would lose ye."

Weakness weighed down her limbs, and she felt as if she would fall asleep and never wake up, but she was hale and whole. "I will be fine, Will. Dinnae fash." Her son continued to suckle at her breast and William stared in awe.

Leaning over, William whispered hotly into her ear. "'Tis a fine thing I had a wee taste of them before he came along. I suspect he will be occupying them from now on." William waggled his brows and Mary felt flushed at the memory of his mouth on her body.

"I suppose he shall," she said with a giggle. "He seems verra eager to feed." Releasing him from her breast, Mary shifted him in her arms, struggling to remove her other nipple from behind her under tunic.

William reached over and pulled the other side down her shoulder, so her son could latch on to the next breast. "Thank ye," she murmured while trying to get him back on. It was not quite as easy as she had suspected it would be but knew with practice, she would master the skill.

"What have ye decided to name him?" William asked, staring at her son's wee face with a grin as wide as she had ever seen. "Will ye name him after his father?"

Looking at William, another round of tears began to blur her eyes, and Mary sniffled, doing her best to choke them back. "Aye, I believe that I shall."

Nodding, William kneeled to the ground and looked her son in his hazel eyes. "Alexander is a fine name for any young man," When he stroked a finger over the bairn's soft cheek, Mary knew she was making the very best decision with her son's name.

"Aye, 'tis," Mary whispered, placing a hand on William's forearm. "But I believe he looks more like a William, dinnae ye think?"

Tearing his gaze away from the bairn, William's eyes widened before crinkling at the corners. "Ye will name him William?"

"Aye. After his father. Ye are his father, arenae ye?" Tilting her head, she cocked a brow at him. The look of surprise mixed with pride in his eyes warmed her heart.

"I am, aye," he answered, his voice croaking as he pushed back emotions. "And I am honored."

"William." Taking his hand in hers, she squeezed it and looked him in the eyes. "I am in love with ye. Ye ken that, aye?"

Shaking his head, he closed his eyes for a moment and then looked at her once more. "Nay, I didnae ken that. Ye never said as much, and I assumed ye still loved Alex."

"I will always love Alex. But I am in love with ye, Will. There is a difference; a verra important difference."

"I love ye, Mary, and I already love wee William more than I have ever loved another. We are a family now." Stroking her cheek, William scanned her face, his bright eyes crinkling at the edges as he seemed to contemplate something. "May I make one request, love?" Mary nodded and looked down at wee William, wondering how she had created such a perfect bairn. "I would like to request that he have Alexander as his second name. After all, he wouldnae be here if not for him."

"William Alexander Keith. I do like the sound of that. Thank ye, Will. Ye are a verra special man. I am sorry I gave ye so much grief before. Ye ken I can be a stubborn woman."

"Well, I am sorry if I ever gave ye cause to give me grief. I ken I am also stubborn. But, I do believe I have met my match, and I look forward to losing many a battle to ye for the rest of my life."

The thought of battle made Mary snap out of the moment, shifting her son in her arms as he finished feeding. "Speaking of battle, I am worried for those at Drum Castle, William. Stephan…"

"Dinnae fash, love. James is on his way there now with orders to command the Hamiltons and Keiths on my behalf. We have learned that Stephan meant to start a feud between the clans, and we will make certain he doesnae succeed."

Breathing deeply, Mary shifted in the bed and propped her head upon his shoulder. "I wish to be away from here. I want to go home."

"I wish to take ye home, but ye just gave birth and yer head wound is still paining ye greatly. What ye need to do is rest. I shall remain here with ye until James returns. I wish to help at Drum, but I willnae leave ye here alone. When it is safe, he will come for us. Then, we can be properly wed and go home to Dunnottar. Would ye like that, my love?"

Her heart lifted, as did the weight on her shoulders. As long as

William was here with her, she could rest easy knowing they were safe. Her entire body ached and the trauma from her attack was still too fresh. "Aye, I trust ye, and I trust James to do all he can to protect Drum. He is headstrong and prideful, but he isnae a fool. He can be trusted to resolve this, I vow."

The prioress arrived once more with two other nuns and fresh linens, ready to clean Mary up after the birth, and she was anxious to be out of her misery. Already, it took all her strength to keep her eyes open. Yawning, Mary handed her bairn to William and sighed. Taking their son carefully, William's face made Mary's stomach flutter. He was so serene, fascinated by wee William.

For now, she was safe. Worry for her kin at Drum still had her in knots, yet there was naught she could do but depend on her arse of an elder brother to do what he did best and command those around him to his will.

Closing her eyes, she drifted away to the sweet sound of her child's coos, knowing he was wrapped in the embrace of a man who truly loved him. Was her experience with Alexander's spirit real or just a machination of her overeager mind to see him one last time? Mayhap it was caused by her head wound. She would likely never know but preferred to believe that he would be with them always.

Chapter Twelve

T HE MOMENT HE arrived back at Drum, his hackles immediately warned him of discontent. There were no sounds of war, but it was quiet: too quiet. Looking around, James saw no sign of the men who usually guarded the perimeter, controlling those who come in and out of the castle. It was midday, and the snow was a blinding blanket of glittering ice as far as he could see, with naught but the towering height of Drum before him.

Riding into the inner bailey and approaching the stables, he saw an elderly man grooming a large, black stud and immediately dismounted, pulling his own horse closer by the reins.

"Good afternoon, Sir James. Have ye come to control yer men?" The man's voice quivered with a lifetime of use, but a tinge of distaste laced his tone.

Though James was several ranks above this man, he knew he had endangered everyone simply by being a raging fool, arriving with the need for recompense upon his sister and the Hamilton good name. Yet, he had not given anyone a chance to speak over his angry demands.

"Indeed, I have, good man. I apologize, but I have forgotten yer name."

Squinting curiously at James, the man cleared his throat. "My name is Finlay, though I suspect I am of no consequence to a man of yer rank. I will only say this: I have lived on Irvine lands the entirety of my five and sixty years on this earth. Many will call me naught but an old eejit, but I have seen much. Yet, never have I seen such a display of pompous power as I witnessed with yer arrival. And may God strike me dead for speaking my mind to a man who outranks me, but if I die today, then I die kenning I said what I must. Ye have endangered my people... Mary's people, ye ken."

Shame fell over James like a heavy, wet blanket, weighing him down. "Have ye a sister, Finlay?"

"Once, aye."

"And what would ye do if ye received a missive that she was ready to bear the child of a man who thought she was well enough to lie with, but not to marry? And that his kin hid it from yers to hide their shame, and hers? What would ye do?"

Licking his old, cracked lips, Finlay shuffled his feet and went back to brushing the black horse standing patiently before him.

"I reckon I would be terribly insulted and out for blood. However, I would have allowed her to speak before carrying her away and dishonoring her before all those she loved. I wouldnae have come with a score of men, but I suppose a lowly man such as me doesnae have such means."

Finlay's point was taken. Nodding, James allowed his shame to seep deep into his bones. He deserved the lashing he was receiving. "What is afoot within the walls?" James jerked his head toward the castle and handed Finlay the reins to his horse.

"Yer men have turned on the Irvines without their laird to command them otherwise. They have released the Douglases from the cellar and currently have our laird, lady, and Sir Reginald held prisoner within their own walls. The rest of yer men have banned up with the Douglases and Keiths, who found a bloodied Irvine plaid and believe them guilty of Sir Brian's murder. Because 'tis the Yule, no fighting has commenced, but I dinnae ken how long that shall last, and though my people have done naught wrong, we are all in danger, surrounded by scores of warriors from other clans with no lairds to command them."

"Ye ken a lot for 'lowly man'," James replied, wondering how he could know so much.

"Aye. I do. Ye think after all these years I dinnae have my sources? That I simply stay within the stables and pet the horses? All the townsfolk are hidden away in their homes while the women and children of the castle are locked in the tower... except for our lady, who is imprisoned." The man scowled. "I refuse to hide. Let them run me through. I will die caring for the creatures I have vowed to protect. I cannae control the fate of men, but I will care for these wee beasts until I die, even if that day is today."

"It shallnae. My thanks, Finlay." James stormed off, having heard enough. He required that information so he understood what he was up against, but time was not on Drum's side, and James needed to get inside and fix what he had helped to create.

Boots cutting a path through the fresh, unpacked snow, James ran toward the entrance of the keep, heart pounding in his chest and regret squeezing his heart like an angry fist, cursed fool that he had been. But he would resolve this, on the honor of his kin.

Attempting to open the door, he growled with frustration when he met resistance. Banging his fist, James roared. "'Tis the Laird of Cadzow! Open the damned doors!"

Only a moment passed before he heard movement on the other side. The door opened slowly and he saw the familiar face of his best warrior. "Let me in, Sir Walter." Not awaiting permission, James rammed the door with his shoulder, and Walter moved aside.

Chaos reigned within the hall, and James searched the room, taking stock of the situation. Shouting curses and threats came from every corner, the Irvine warriors held against the wall of their own home while Hamiltons, Keiths, and Douglases wielded swords and shouted profanities in tandem. It was hard to distinguish the clustered threats and curses, but James understood enough to know that a feud had begun and it was ready to turn violent.

Enough of this. Putting his fingers in his mouth, James released a deafening whistle that made every man in the hall go silent immediately and turn in his direction. "Stand down!" he roared, pulling out his own sword and narrowing his hazel gaze on all the men. "I speak on behalf of the Laird of Dunnottar, as well, who is at the kirk attending my sister. He sent me in his stead to command his men. Put yer swords away and let the Irvines go!"

The Keiths hesitated, but his Hamilton men obeyed. "Our laird wouldnae ask us to stand down if he kenned the truth! An Irvine killed our man!" one of the Keiths shouted, refusing to comply. The others nodded and grumbled their agreement, keeping the Irvines captive and refusing to move.

"Aye, 'tis the truth." Archibald Douglas stepped forward, looking as pompous as ever with a smirk that resembled a cat who had caught a mouse. "The plaid was found covered in blood. 'Tis undeniable evidence of treachery. The Irvines dishonored yer sister, my daughter, and their peace with the Keiths. They couldnae prevent the spilling of blood between their clans for even the Yuletide." Archibald spat on the ground and walked slowly toward James. "All Lady Elizabeth went though to achieve peace between the Irvines and clans, being pawned from father to son to son, was for naught. And yer sister paid the price with the bastard she carries. My men willnae stand down. 'Tis time to rid this land of the Irvines and form our own alliance."

The Douglas men nodded and shouted their consent, shaking their swords and pointing them more forcefully at the necks of the unarmed Irvine men.

"Yer men have no honor, taking arms against unarmed men," James scowled, but the Black Douglas only shrugged, proving to be the dishonorable cad James had always suspected him to be. "Why do the Douglases draw arms? I dinnae see any cause."

Archibald's face turned red as his bluster piqued. "They invited us here for the Yule, only to lock me away in that dank cellar on a false charge of murder! My men were forced down there and held captive. This is naught more than justice! My daughter was humiliated!"

Stepping even closer to the Douglas, James gritted his teeth and clenched his sword until his knuckles cracked. "Listen carefully, all of ye!" he demanded and then focused once more on Archibald. "Do ye think to blame others for her treatment when ye made her bleed? I cannae command the Douglases, but I can command the Keiths, by order of their laird who will have their hides if they dinnae comply!" His vision blurred from the rage he felt, much of it directed at himself for having contributed to the mess.

"Aye. We ken an Irvine killed a Keith. Yer laird kens this, as well." The Keiths shouted and raised their swords, demanding revenge and blood. "Silence!" The room verily shook with the deep command of his voice, and every man quieted once more. "We also ken which man did it. Stephan Irvine was working with The Douglas to turn everyone against the Irvines!"

The crowd of warriors became restless once more, but an air of uncertainty now resounded in their mutterings. The Irvine men did not seem at all shocked to hear that Stephan was involved in such a plot, though their faces of contempt proved their disapproval of the man.

"That is a bald-faced lie! I should kill ye where ye stand for spouting such nonsense!"

"The man confessed it himself while he was attacking my sister! He wrote that missive and mentioned the kirk, kenning I would show up and take her away! He killed Brian in his sleep after he heard him rejecting Marjorie. Not only did it place the blame on the Douglases, but it also was naught more than a distraction, so when I showed up to take Mary away, he could sneak out and follow behind. But The Douglas kenned this, didnae he? He kenned he would be blamed for the murder. That gave him a reason to turn on the Irvines. He kenned the bloody plaid would be found, making the Keiths turn on the Irvines, as well. The Hamiltons would turn on the Irvines for dishonoring the sister of their laird, and the Irvines would be outnumbered and easy prey!"

James looked around and was pleased to see the men listening, turning their hot gazes toward the Douglases. "Their treachery kens no bounds and I command the Hamiltons and Keiths to stand down from the Irvines and turn yer gazes and swords on the true enemy amongst us: Archibald Douglas!"

James pointed his sword at the man's throat and, for once, Archibald had the mind to stay silent. Dropping his sword, the Douglas put his hands up, his graying hairline rising with his brows. "Ye have no proof of any of that. Yer word against mine. I ken nothing about any of that mad Irvine's schemes, nor any knowledge of his association with the Douglas Clan. Ye have made a grave mistake accusing me of such a plot, lad. I dinnae care if ye are a laird, a baron, or the bloody king! I have all the power of Scotland and England backing me up. I am untouchable. Slit my throat and ye shall be hanged for treason, for I am royalty!" he shouted, his jowls shaking and his face turning almost purple. He was caught in a conspiracy and James simply held the sword steady, not frightened by this old blithering goat.

"So ye will tell me that Stephan Irvine isnae yer nephew? That ye didnae pin yer assassination of the king's eldest son on yer own brother's head, causing him to be cast aside? Ye didnae tell Stephan that ye would restore his place among the Black Douglases if he helped to cause a ripple in the fragile peace these clans have recently established, wishing to weaken them all and eventually take them down?" James guessed on most of his accusations, but it all made sense, and based on the wide-eyed look of Archibald who attempted to hide his shaking hands at his side, he knew he had figured out the truth.

"How dare ye accuse me of such foul deeds! I have nothing to do with Stephan or the death of the old king's son... who was my wife's brother! And I certainly had nothing to do with turning clans against the Irvines! They accomplished that on their own."

"That isnae the truth."

A middle-aged man with long, red hair pulled back into a queue and wearing a Douglas plaid draped over his shoulder stepped forward, head held high, eyes glaring at his laird. "My name is Roger Galloway, Laird Hamilton. I am the messenger for Sir Archibald. All these years, I have had to deliver one missive after another that led to skirmishes and bloodshed that now rest upon my soul, coating my hands. I ken I didnae write them, nor ken of their contents, but I always kenned they were filled with bile and lies, turning clans against one another to weaken their alliances and create wars over power. I can no longer stand the stain upon my soul. I ken the truth of it. Sir Archibald told Stephan Irvine to write the missive to ye. Vowed to offer him sanctuary on his lands. Stephan's father was the laird's younger brother who was banished for something he didnae do. We all ken it."

The shouting in the hall grew louder by the moment as outrage heightened. The swords held by the Keiths and Hamiltons pulled away from the Irvines, now focused on the Douglases. James kept his own weapon steadily held at the throat of the man who conspired against the Irvines whose only fault was welcoming Archibald into their home.

"We demand revenge for the death of Brian!" one Keith warrior shouted, raising his sword in the air. His words were met with a round of approval from his kin who filled the hall.

"An eye for an eye!" another man shouted, and the Keiths began to crowd around Archibald and his men, determined to seek justice for their loss.

"Hold yer weapons, men. 'Tis still the Yule. We have seen enough blood and hatred. Surround the Douglas Clan. Irvine men, head down to the cellar with me to release yer laird and lady. Walter!" James called to his finest warrior, who nodded and pushed through the crush of men to arrive by his side and hear his command. "Watch this bastard for me. Dinnae take yer eyes nor yer sword away from him. Where is Miss Douglas?"

"She is in the tower with the other women, my laird."

"Good. Stephan Irvine is on the loose, likely headed toward Douglas lands. We cannae reach him before he arrives, but we can handle the bastard before us now. I will allow Robert to decide his fate." Sending a warning scowl in Archibald's direction, James walked away, knowing Walter would not let him down.

Walking up to Roger, James placed an arm on his shoulder and nodded. "Ye were verra brave to speak up. Ye have saved lives on this day. I ken ye will need protection, and I welcome ye to live on Hamilton lands. We can use all the trustworthy men we can get."

"Thank ye, my laird," the man said and bowed. "I couldnae stand it any longer. I accept yer offer and ken ye will be a fairer leader than any Black Douglas."

Looking at the rest of the men, James placed a hand over his quickly beating heart, tightly gripping his sword with his other. "I have failed. I fell into the trap and put everyone at risk. I'm not worthy of yer forgiveness, nor yer allegiance, but I ask that ye do this one thing for me. Help me release the prisoners below. I shall face whatever fate Laird Drum sees fit for disrupting his home during the Yule and endangering his kin."

The Irvines nodded and stepped away from the wall, shooting daggers at the other men who had held them captive before grabbing their swords, stacked in the nearby corner. James followed as the men led him across the hall and around the screens separating the room from the kitchens. The emptiness of the room was eerie enough, but the pot left unstirred as the stew within bubbled and burned spoke of a castle in a frenzy, and James was sorry to have been involved in the mayhem he had created.

"The cellar is down this way, Sir William," one of the Irvine knights said, opening a door that led down to the basement area of the tower.

"Is there an outer entrance?"

"Aye. There is a flight of stairs just outside the tower that leads to the basement from the inner bailey. There are men from Douglas and Keith guarding that entrance, as well."

Looking behind him, he saw a score of men awaiting their turn to release their laird and lady, ready to fight any man in the way. James divided the men behind him into two groups, then addressed the first half. "Gather my men and go around to the outside entrance. We will enter through here and call off the guards. If they dinnae comply, we will need to have our swords ready." Nodding, the men took off through another door that led outside.

James began to step down when one warrior grabbed a lit candle from the kitchens. "We will be needing some light. 'Tis naught but a long, dark corridor before we reach the cellars." The candle was nearly burned down to the base of its brass holder, another indication that the kitchens had been quickly abandoned. Nodding, James took the candle and stepped into the dark first, the men following in a single file line.

A long, slim corridor stood before him, stretching for several feet before curving to the left. James followed the path, keeping one hand on the hilt of his sword as he rounded the dark corner. The air was nearly freezing, the sting of the chill nipping at his ears, cheeks, and nose with every step.

Holding the small bit of candle up and praying it did not suddenly die out, he saw a corridor that seemed to go on as far as his eyes could see, several doors lining both sides. "Which door is the cellar?" he whispered to the men behind him.

"'Tis the verra furthest down, Sir William. The verra last door on the left. There are two levels to the cellar. Once ye enter, ye will see yet another set of stairs. They are being held in the bottom level. They have no light or warmth," the man replied with concern in his tone.

Cursing under his breath, James continued down the hall, worried for Elizabeth and the bairn she carried. Finally reaching the end of what felt like a tunnel leading to a cave, William slowly opened the last door and entered a small, square room where a few animal carcasses hung from metal hooks attached to the ceiling. This room was just as cold at the corridor leading to it, which he was glad of at the moment. It properly stored the meat from going foul, a smell he was not eager to endure.

Holding the candle up, he saw the stairway across the room in the corner, and moved around the carcass of a boar, determined to get down those stairs and into the cellar.

As he made the final turn of the rounded staircase, James was met by two warriors guarding the way and swiftly drew his sword, hearing the men behind him do the same, the echo of unsheathed steal bouncing off the walls. The men before him wore the Douglas plaid, and James hoped they would not make this harder than necessary.

"The building is surrounded and yer laird is held captive in the hall. Ye can stand aside or be cut down. 'Tis yer choice." The two men looked behind James, keeping calm looks on their faces before looking at one another, deciding their next move.

Shrugging, one man moved to the side. "I care not to die without lying with my wife once more, nor do I like keeping a lady locked in the cold darkness below."

The other man moved aside as well, smart enough to know he was outnumbered and had no better options. "Here." Putting his hand out, the man brandished a long, metal key. "This belongs to the lady." The Irvine warrior behind him took the key and the Douglas men stepped away. When the lock clicked and the door swung open with a deafening groan, William stepped forward, holding his sword in front of him.

"Who enters?" Robert's angry voice echoed through the room, but even with the candle, James still could not see him. Taking a few more steps inside, James turned in a slow circle, looking for any sign of the laird and lady.

"'Tis James Hamilton."

"Och, have ye come to finish the job then? Ye ken, I had expected better of ye Hamiltons than to side with the bloody Black Douglases. Ye can kill me like a coward while I am tied up and unarmed. But I vow if ye touch my wife, I will come back from the dead and cut ye limb from cursed limb!"

"Rob, nay! Dinnae make things worse." Elizabeth hissed in the dark.

"Ye must kill me if ye plan on killing my brother, for I dinnae wish to be saddled with the running of this place. Then I would need to take a wife, and I fear that is akin to death for me." That must be the voice of Reginald Irvine. Though James had not been formally introduced to him, his reputation as a witty lover of women and lighthearted banter preceded him.

Stepping in a few feet further, James finally saw them in the corner, all bound by their arms and legs, sitting in the furthest corner. Even the slightest bit of light made them all squint and turn away, and he saw Elizabeth shivering against Robert. The bastards had not even given the lady the courtesy of a plaid or a shawl.

"I am here to get ye out. The Keiths and Hamiltons have been called off and are now surrounding the Douglases." James took a moment to fill them in on what he had discovered about Brian's murder, and Stephan Irvines role in the events before fleeing to Douglas lands.

"That son of a bitch. My father allowed him to live on our lands, and this is how he repays us? We treated him like kin," Robert spat, clenching his teeth. Obvious disappointment and betrayal laced his words.

"I dinnae believe Stephan cares for anyone or anything, other than himself. He will do all he can to have Mary. He attacked her at the kirk, but we arrived in time to save her before he fled."

"Where is Mary? Is she all right?" Elizabeth cried, and James was not certain if the quiver in her voice was from the cold or fear.

"She is at the kirk with William. She went into labor and is being cared for by the prioress who is also a midwife. She was verra well when I had to leave. Will stayed to make certain she was safe and sent me to command his men." Coming closer, James put his sword down and pulled a dagger out of his boot. "I am going to cut yer binds," he assured them all.

"Nay! Mary is alone, giving birth without me? I vowed I would be with her when her time came!"

"I am sorry, my lady. I cannae stress my regret for my previous behavior enough. Much has happened since the night before." With a grunt of exertion, James cut through the remainder of ropes around her feet and moved over to Robert, continuing his conversation with Elizabeth. "I cannae make up for what I have done to her. But I ken William will allow her to visit Drum and attend to ye when ye give birth. Perhaps that will please ye both."

"What the devil?" As soon as Robert's ropes were cut, he hopped to his feet with a groan and reached out to Elizabeth, embracing her and rubbing his hands over her body to warm her chilled flesh. "Lizzie... what is he saying, love?"

James was occupied cutting the ropes off Reginald next, but he heard the confusion in Robert's tone and grimaced. Robert had not known yet either. James had now told both her brother and husband before she had, and he felt like a bloody arse.

"Well... I didnae wish ye to ken yet. 'Tis early days still, Rob. And I certainly didnae wish for ye to find out while we were down here."

She looked at James and narrowed her eyes before looking back at Robert. "Anything can happen."

"I am going to be a father?" he croaked. A smile widened on his face, the dim light of the candle casting a shaky shadow over his elated features. "I am going to be a father!" he roared into the darkness, the sound reverberating off the walls.

"Rob, haud yer wheesht!" Elizabeth slapped her hand over his mouth and shook her head. "The bats hibernate in this cellar in the winter, dinnae ye ken? 'Tis not an easy task to awake them, but if ye do, we shall be swarmed!"

Reginald stretched his neck when he stood, wiping debris from the back of his breeches and rubbing his sore backside. "I am to be an uncle?" he asked. "Again? Mary is having Alexander's child as we speak, and ye are with child, as well? The Irvine Clan will have some braw new warriors, I ken." Reginald grinned and looked at James. "Ye are fortunate ye come bearing good tiding, or else I would consider running ye through for the way ye treated our Mary."

James stared at Reginald, torn between telling the man to mind his own business, explaining his behavior, or apologizing altogether. He had acted brashly, aye, but she was his Mary, also. He was her guardian and he had done what he thought best to keep her and the bairn safe. His apology was owed specifically to Mary and he would continue to make amends on her behalf, but none of that concerned Sir Reginald Irvine who seemed to share opinions about things whether invited to or not.

"Those bastards tied up my wife while she carries a bairn!" Robert hissed and pulled her near, cradling Elizabeth in his embrace, swallowing her up with his size.

"Rob, they didnae ken I was with child," she mumbled against his chest.

"That isnae the point! Ye are Lady of Drum and deserve respect. They can tie me and Reg up and leave us to the mice, but not my fair lady wife!"

Reginald grimaced at his brother. "Och. I am glad to ken how much ye regard me," he said dryly. It seemed Reginald took nothing seriously, which made him both endearing and frustrating.

"Archibald is up in the hall being watched by my men. I called off the Hamiltons and Keiths, but the Douglases are still a threat. It's up to ye how ye wish to handle the Back Douglas." Just as he spoke the words, shouts rang out from the side of the cellar, and Robert's head turned.

"That is the entrance from the outside. Are there men there?"

"Aye, Douglas' men were guarding that side of the cellar. Yer men must have just found them. Robert, take Elizabeth through the corridor and deal with the men in the hall. Yer men can clear the way and we will meet ye there. Reginald, how are ye with a dagger?" James asked, flashing his blade, knowing the men were both unarmed.

"None better." Reginald took the dagger and flipped it in his hand, catching it by the handle.

"That remains to be seen." Unsheathing his sword, James shrugged his head toward the back entrance and Reginald followed.

"Ye are brave to command me in my own home, Sir James. But, aye, Elizabeth must stay safe, and I willnae leave her alone in this cellar. I am sorry ye must fight without me, but I ken ye both can handle it." The men who came with James through the corridor surrounded their laird and lady, determined to see them to safety as they all went through the inside door, disappearing into the darkness.

"Are ye ready?" Reginald asked, but he did not await an answer before opening the door, the brightness of the afternoon sun streaming in and causing James to suffer a moment of temporary blindness before his eyes adjusted. Running through with Reginald, James held his sword high and ready to strike.

Several Douglas guards struggled with the Irvines, yet some had already been felled. Seeing one man fighting off two Douglas warriors,

James growled and jumped into the fight, clashing his sword against the enemy just as it swung toward the Irvine warrior's chest.

With a grunt, the Douglas man took a step back, nearly losing his balance in the powdery snow before making eye contact with James and scowling, thrusting his sword toward James' gut. Swerving to the right, he successfully dodged the blow before swiftly spinning on his heels and slashing the man's arm, causing him to shout in pain and drop into the snow along with his weapon. Blood painted the snow as it oozed from the man's right forearm. It was not a killing blow, nor was it meant to be. These men were acting on the command of their laird, just as his own men were. There were moments when a life must be taken, but this was not one of them.

The Irvine warrior nodded to James in thanks, then turned to fight another man. Turning around, James saw Reginald stab a man in the thigh just as he was charging at James' back. Had Reginald not been there, James may never have had his chance to truly make amends to his sister. The serious glower on Reginald's face was a completely different side of the man James had briefly met before, and a new respect for him formed. He was a man who used his humor and charm to lighten his outlook on life, but when it came to battle and loyalty, Reginald Irvine was a man who could be trusted to have your back... and save your arse.

Slapping Reginald on the back, James stopped and took a breath when he saw that no more Douglases were coming at them. Keith and Irvine men stood in a circle around the wounded Douglas warriors and awaited a command from James.

"Lead us to the hall, men. Robert is on his way there now to deal with The Douglas." Nodding, the men huffed for breath but ran as fast as they could through the snow with Reginald and James following.

The door to the keep was wide open and James walked in behind Reginald, seeing Robert and Elizabeth standing in front of Archibald, who was surrounded by warriors from three other clans and no choice but to surrender if he was intelligent.

"Ye put us all at risk, Douglas! We invited ye here for the Yule and this is our thanks?" Robert spat and clung to Elizabeth who held her ground and kept her head high. No man would suspect the woman had just left the cold darkness of a cellar she had been bound in for hours. "Ye conspired with Stephan to kill a Keith and put my people in danger."

"Yer daughter is staying here with us, Archibald." Elizabeth straightened her spine and wagged her finger at the man. "Ye mistreat her and use her as a pawn for an alliance, but the truth is, ye dinnae care for peace. Ye simply wished to be rid of her. She may stay here on Irvine lands where she will be fostered by me personally and learn how to be a lady of a keep and have some proper manners. And when the time is right, I vow she will have a good match for a husband. As it is, she is not prepared to be a wife or a lady, and ye ken it."

Archibald shrugged and rolled his eyes. "Keep the bitch. Mayhap she will be of more use to ye than she was to me. 'Tis a fine thing the tournament was canceled, so no man was saddled with the lass."

James shot daggers at the man, pitying his wee daughter for being treated as naught but cattle to be traded, and grateful she was tucked away in the tower where his cruel words could not be heard. Archibald Douglas had earned his reputation through the years, upholding his black legacy, but never had his soul appeared darker than it did now.

Stepping up to Archibald, Robert gripped the hilt of his sword until his knuckles turned white. "Ye dinnae ken how badly I wish to rid the world of ye here and now. But, 'tis still the Yule, and enough blood has been shed because of ye. Ye are fortunate I find myself in a fair mood. My men are all safe and accounted for, and my women and children are safe in the tower. And, I have just discovered that I am to be a father." Robert looked behind him and smiled like a fool to his wife, who flushed and held her reddening cheeks.

The warriors in the hall cheered and stomped their feet loudly, letting out whistles and words of congratulations to Robert and Elizabeth, who simply nodded and smiled in response. James watched these people and understood why they meant so much to Mary. They were fierce, but they were fair. The Irvines had taken care of her and though one had planted a bastard in her belly, James understood now that Mary was no wee lass. She had loved and been loved before tragedy struck, and she had suffered enough for it. Now, she had William Keith. And though finding him with his paws all over his sister had been enough to make James nearly slay the man, he had come to understand that theirs was also true love. Any man who would fight to wed a woman carrying another man's child was a good man, indeed. Mary had loved and been loved twice, where James had never known such an emotion. Who was he to judge her for his inability to feel more than lust for a woman?

Clearing his throat, Robert put his hand up to silence the crowd. "There are still five days left of the Yule, and I intend to celebrate them peacefully with my kin, which includes the Keiths and the Hamiltons," he said, looking at James before looking back at The Douglas. "Ye arenae welcome on my lands as long as ye shall live. This is yer only warning. If yer toe crosses onto my lands, I shall remove it, along with yer head. Get yer men and hie yer arse off my land before I change my mind! And ken that this isnae over and the clans will all be seeking justice for Brian when ye least expect it!" Robert roared so loudly that many in the crowd jumped, the sound taking everyone by surprise as the walls reverberated.

"Aye! Ye dinnae kill a Keith and walk away unscathed!" a man shouted from the crowd, shaking his fist while heads nodded and eyes shot daggers all around the hall. It would be a miracle if The Douglas made it back to his lands in one piece at this point.

Tugging on his surcoat, Archibald Douglas simply raised a brow and turned away, having no desire to apologize and knowing he was outnumbered. "Ye shall regret this treatment of me, Irvine," the man threatened as he walked toward the entrance of the keep.

"I dare say I willnae." Robert walked toward the door and watched as his warriors followed the Douglases into the inner bailey and toward the stables. When they were out of sight, he slammed the doors and turned to the remaining people. "Lizzie, 'tis safe to allow the women and children out of the tower now. Please tell Marjorie to report to me in my solar to discuss her new… life. As for the rest of ye, I apologize for allowing a Black Douglas to enter our keep, but we shallnae allow it to ruin our Yule any further. Mary is at the kirk birthing Alexander's child. I wonder if perhaps ye all would be willing to go on a wee journey? Since she cannae travel back to us, we can bring the Yule to her."

The men all cheered, hollering their agreement, and James felt pride for his sister and gratitude for the Irvines. She was truly cherished by so many, most of all him, though he had done a poor job of showing it. Walking up to Robert, James put a hand on the man's shoulder. "I was wrong about ye. Mary is right, as usual. Dinnae tell her I said that, or I shall lie through my teeth."

Laughing, Robert shook his head and leaned in closer to James. "I ken all too well about women being correct more often than not. Yer secret is safe with me. By nightfall, we shall all arrive at the kirk and have a Yule celebration together with Mary. And mayhap, ye shall have a wee niece or nephew to greet." Patting him on the back, Robert walked away and James smiled like a bloody fool. He was going to be an uncle, and he had Alexander Irvine to thank for that… even if it pained him to admit it.

CHAPTER THIRTEEN

SLOWLY AWAKENING FROM the deepest sleep in her entire life, Mary gasped and sat up straight in her bed, head pounding and body aching. "My bairn!"

"He is safe, my love, and so are ye." Rubbing her eyes, the blur of sleep slowly disappeared and focused on a sight that took her breath away. William sat in the corner of the room holding their new son. It seemed all her fear and pain melted away that very moment, and her heart felt weightless.

"How long was I asleep?" she asked, stretching and yawning. Her head still hurt, but the throbbing had lessened as the hours passed.

"The bell just rang for vespers. Ye have been asleep for three hours."

"Oh, my. I am verra sorry. How is wee William?" She saw her bairn with his eyes closed, but he stirred in William's arms, his head turning from side to side.

"He has been asleep as long as ye have. Dinnae apologize. Ye have had a rough time and needed the rest, but I do believe he is ready to feed again." Standing up, William looked down at their bairn and smiled widely. "How are ye feeling?"

"I feel a wee bit better. I just wish we kenned where Stephan was. I feel my skin crawling when I think of his hands on me. I worry that he is watching me."

Leaning over, William kissed her forehead and gently handed their son to her and helped her prepare to feed him. "He isnae here or anywhere near here. I am certain he went to Douglas lands. He will never touch ye again, and I will kill him if I ever set eyes on him. But ye dinnae need to be fashed. I am certain Robert will seek him out after the Yule."

Sighing, Mary relaxed and enjoyed the sensation of being a new mother, nursing her wee bairn in her arms. He was so small and light in her arms. After several moments of nursing him and wondering why William seemed to be anxious, pacing the room and shuffling his feet, Mary looked up at him and forced a smile. "Is something bothering ye, William?" Self-doubt dug its claws into her mind, plaguing her with a sudden lack of confidence. Was William having second thoughts about raising wee William or marrying her? Mayhap she was becoming more trouble than she was worth. Though she was usually a proud woman, never had she felt weaker and more vulnerable than she did now.

Walking over to her, William touched her arm and his features softened, a wide smile spreading across his lips. "Nay, my love. That is just the thing. Nothing is bothering me. Never has my life felt righter." Sitting down on the edge of the bed, William stroked her cheek. "Ye are so loved, Mary. Not only by me but by everyone who kens ye. I was an arse to ye, and I am verra sorry. Will ye marry me? Here? Today?"

Heart palpitating in her chest, Mary's eyes widened and she shifted in the bed. "Here? William, I want to marry ye more than aught, and we are in a kirk filled with priests who can perform the ceremony, but I wish to be married surrounded by our kin." She frowned and hoped she was not hurting him or making him feel rejected. Truly, she would marry him this very second if she could.

"Is that yer only concern, my love? Ye would marry me here today if ye had yer kin?"

"Well, aye. I would. I would need help getting ready, for I cannae marry ye in my shift," she added dryly. "But, aye, I would marry ye."

"Do ye think ye are strong enough to get out of bed and get dressed long enough for a ceremony?" He was asking rather odd and specific questions. Mary raised a brow at him and touched her head, realizing someone had removed her makeshift wrap at some point while she slept. Though tender, the wound had stopped bleeding and her restful sleep had served to stop the incessant pounding in her skull.

"I suppose so, aye. I feel rather well considering how awful I felt before I slept, but I am certain I will be weak and not last long. Why are ye asking? I suppose it would do me good to stretch my legs, but…" Leaning in, William kissed her on the lips and stopped her from finishing her words.

"I am asking because there are a few of yer kin here to see ye, love." William rose from the bed. Mary watched him walk to the door, her brow creasing with confusion while wee William yawned in her arms.

When the door opened, Mary gasped when she saw James and Elizabeth peek their heads through the doors. "Oh, my!" Mary was speechless. Did they come all this way just to see her? When they saw the bairn, both stepped in, Elizabeth loudly squealing and making him stir in his sleep. Covering her mouth, Elizabeth shot her an apologetic look before gently sweeping him out of her arms without asking. Mary was glad for the reprieve, but still unsure of what exactly was going on.

"'Tis a wee braw laddie named William!" William announced, sounding like a proud father, and Mary wished to kiss him all over. How had she ever rejected this man who was already the most affectionate and protective father?

"A son? How wonderful, Mary." James smiled and came closer,

touching Mary's arm. "My wee sister, I cannae tell ye how much I regret my treatment of ye. I do hope ye will forgive me in time."

"That depends on why ye are here and what ye have to report from Drum. Is everyone well?" Dread made her belly drop and her vision go blurry. "Have ye come bearing ill tidings?"

"Nay," Elizabeth whispered and rocked wee William in her arms, staring down at his face. "All is well at Drum. James saved us, ye ken. The Douglases have left and shall never return unless they wish to face Robert's wrath. Only Marjorie has remained and will stay with us where she is safe and can learn to be a proper lady," she added slowly.

Mary looked at James and sighed, no longer wishing to argue with her brother. She thought she was going to be killed by Stephan only hours before. Life was too short and precious to worry over the past. "Then ye are forgiven, Brother. I only care now about my son and my kin. I have nothing to be ashamed of, for all I have done in this life has brought me the greatest joy in the end. As for Marjorie, I think ye did right allowing her to stay. She is rotten, but she deserves better than the treatment she receives from her father. I ken she will flourish under yer care." Contentment was stronger than any pain her body was feeling and, suddenly, she felt as if she could dance on air. "Though I am pleased to see ye, I wonder what has brought ye here during the Yule. Shouldnae ye be having a feast and celebrating?"

Mary looked at William and smiled, passing wee William into James' arms. Hesitating, James went white as he carefully cradled his new nephew, gently holding his wee fuzzy head and looking at him as if he were made of ancient parchment and likely to crumble to pieces.

"Aye, Mary! Ye are right that we must be grateful for our blessings and celebrate the Yule with our kin. The problem is that three verra important members of our kin are here, and we cannae celebrate without ye, ye ken."

Mary looked from James to Elizabeth to William and back to Elizabeth. "I am afraid I dinnae understand. Mayhap I hit my head harder than I thought."

Frowning, Elizabeth grabbed Mary's hand and scowled. "Stephan is a coward and a bastard. He has been banned from the clan and stripped of his good name. If he wishes to deal with the Black Douglases, then he can be one! Curse the man for putting his hands on ye. We will make him pay for his sins."

"I am all right, Lizzie. Now do tell me what ye are speaking about before I decide I truly am daft."

"Well, ye wee fool. Dinnae ye understand? We brought the Yule to ye!" Now Mary was certain that she suffered from a head injury. First, she saw Alexander's spirit, and now she was hearing tall tales.

"Ye brought the Yule here... to a kirk? I dinnae understand, nor do I suspect the priests will be glad of it."

"That is where ye are wrong, Mary." William took her other hand and caressed it with his fingers. "At first, they were reluctant, aye, but once Elizabeth explained why they came, the priests were most pleased to have so many Scots in their kirk to celebrate mass and the Yule. The priest that Stephan stole the key from was found, injured by a stab wound in the chest and nearly frozen to death near the stables, but they have revived him and believe he will survive. It appears we all have much to be thankful for. Although, we dinnae ken how we shall all fit. And there is no food for a feast, but plenty of ale and whisky... all a Scotsman needs, ye ken."

"I am verra relieved the priest was found and Stephan didnae succeed in killing a holy man. His soul is cursed enough. But... exactly how many more people are here in the kirk from Drum?"

"Why dinnae ye get dressed and we will help ye out of bed so ye can find out. Hopefully, ye can stand on yer feet long enough to say yer vows," William said with a wink and a smirk that would have made her knees buckle if she was not already in bed.

"Vows? Ye are all mad, I ken it!"

"Didnae I ask ye if ye would marry me? Ye said ye would if ye had yer kin. Well, ye do." A smug look transformed William's handsome face, and his reddish-blond hair glittered in the light of the candles, making Mary wish to run her hands through it.

"Aye... but... I cannae get married in my ruined and torn dress. Ye ken I wish to marry ye, Will, but I also wish to look like a true bride, not a disheveled, homeless lass!"

Walking toward the door, Elizabeth cracked it open and stuck her head into the hall and then looked back at Mary. "I cannae agree more. I wonder if ye ken who ye are speaking to. I am the woman who organized a tournament in two days' time. Ye dinnae think I can plan a wedding in two hours?" Scoffing, Elizabeth stepped aside and Matilda walked in, carrying a large roll of cloth and wearing the grandest of smiles.

"Tilda?" Mary rubbed her eyes and sat up straight in the bed. "Ye came, as well?"

"Och, Mary. We all did. Dinnae ye ken how much we love ye? And before ye go giving me undue praise, I must tell ye that this was all yer brother's plan."

James slowly looked up from the bairn and cracked a small smile, shrugging as if it were nothing at all to bring the Yule and a wedding to the very sister he had left in a kirk to give birth.

"I have much to atone for, Mary. I cannae take back all I said or did. Ye gave birth without the Lady of Drum by yer side. 'Twas Robert's plan to bring the Yule to ye, but aye, I thought it would mayhap be a gesture of goodwill if I showed my support for yer wedding to William."

Tears unwillingly slid down Mary's face, and she wiped them away, only for more to form. "Oh, James. Thank ye. This means more to me than aught." Sniffling, she wiped more tears away and narrowed her eyes. "So, ye willnae be taking away by bairn, after all, aye?"

Gasping, Mary looked at James and smacked his arm, making certain not to disturb wee William. "Ye threatened to take her bairn?

Ye are fortunate Mary is so kindhearted. I daresay I would never forgive such a thing!"

Waving it away, Mary shook her head. "He wouldnae. I ken it. He is all hot air and bluster."

"I am, aye," James said with a contrite look. "I was an arse and will regret my words for a lifetime." The way he looked at her son made Mary's heart melt with a love and happiness that threatened to spill over.

"We all have regrets. I treated Will horribly and insulted him at every opportunity. I dinnae feel worthy of his love, but if he wishes to marry me today, I shall, even if I must wear a torn and muddy dress."

"Ye willnae have to," Matilda said and stepped forward, placing the roll of cloth on the bed across Mary's legs. "I do hope this will do." Unfolding the cloth, shimmering light blue silk caught the light of the flickering candles and Mary gasped, clutching her chest. "My mother's wedding dress! But, how did ye ken where to find it?"

"Yer brother informed us that when ye left Cadzow all those years ago with yer mother, she had placed her dress at the bottom of yer trunk. Matilda pressed out all the wrinkles and let out the hem a bit. 'Tis verra beautiful and will make ye look like a queen, I vow." Elizabeth smiled and picked up a matching ribbon from within the roll of cloth. "And this is my ribbon. I thought it matched verra well and would be honored if ye tied it up in yer hair with..." Pausing, Elizabeth searched the satchel tied to the side of her belt and pulled out a fresh piece of mistletoe. "This. I have much of it all around the hall, ye ken." Elizabeth rolled her eyes, and Mary was torn between laughing and crying. Tears of joy rolled down her cheeks, and she choked back a sob.

Stepping forward, William looked at the mistletoe and shook his head. "If ye dinnae mind, I ken 'tis a wee bit shriveled, but mayhap ye would consider this sprig of mistletoe instead?" Reaching into his surcoat, William pulled out a necklace with a small leather bag attached to the end. When he opened it up, he pulled out the piece of mistletoe Mary had given him just two days ago at the joust. It seemed a lifetime had passed since that day. But knowing that William had been treasuring it and keeping it near his heart all this time made Mary burst out in a new round of tears.

"I dinnae deserve any of ye," she cried. "Thank ye, for everything."

"Bollocks. Ye deserve the world, Mary, and I will spend every day of my life making certain ye have it." William picked up her hand and brought it to his lips, kissing it gently while she just looked at him in awe before looking at her child and loved ones surrounding her. They had gone through so much to be here, to plan this. Her throat constricted with emotions as she tried to push them down.

"If ye dinnae mind, we have scores of Irvines, Hamiltons, and Keiths in the cathedral awaiting a bride and bridegroom. The men need to leave so we may get Mary ready," Matilda demanded, never one to linger on sentiments.

Shooing the men out as James carried wee William, Matilda shut the door behind them and turned to look at Mary and flashed a grin Mary knew all too well. "Are ye ready to become William's wife? Or did we just force ye into something ye dinnae want? Say the word, and I will hie his arse back to Dunnottar with naught but Marjorie for company."

Laughing, Mary nodded and shifted in the bed. "I do want this, Tilda. More than I ever suspected I would. Ye were right about yer brother, Lizzie. I have grown to love him verra much."

"Aye, I ken it. I heard what was seen when James arrived, and though I am pleased that my match worked as well as I believed, I can do without the details, ye ken."

Blushing, Mary put her hand on her cheeks. "I vow never to bore ye with the details."

"Good. Now, let's make a bride of ye!" Elizabeth said with excitement and both women surrounded Mary, giggling like wee lasses.

Mary closed her eyes and enjoyed Matilda's careful and gentle hand as she brushed Mary's hair and hid her wound. Though her days seemed to blend together, her body ached, and she vowed she could sleep for three days straight, Mary looked at her mother's wedding dress and all her worries, pain, and tiredness vanished. Today, she would marry William Keith, who turned out to be a gem of a man hidden beneath his rough, hard exterior. Once he showed who he was inside, he glowed with love and loyalty, and she would treasure him and the day Elizabeth sat them beneath the mistletoe until her last breath.

WAITING FOR MARY in front of her chamber door, William paced back and forth, anxious to wed the only woman he would ever love. She was everything he could ever want, and she loved him despite all his faults and mistakes.

"Ye will wear a hole in the stone floors if ye keep up yer pacing," James said from behind him, holding wee William as he slept.

"I wish to marry yer sister before she changes her mind," William scoffed, adjusting the Keith plaid resting across his shoulders just over his surcoat.

"She would be a fool to." That was the most William could ever expect as a compliment from her brother so, nodding, he decided to accept it.

When the door opened, Mary stood before him with Elizabeth and Matilda helping to hold her up. He knew she was weak and tired, but before him stood the most beautiful woman he had ever seen, with her red waves carefully twisted up to hide her wound, a blue ribbon and his mistletoe delicately woven through. Her mother's blue silk dress fit her as if it had been created just for her, with long, flowing sleeves that went past her wrists and a neckline high enough to modestly cover her breasts. Her Hamilton plaid was draped and tied expertly across her shoulder to show her clan pride and he could not wait to see her wrapped up in nothing but his Keith plaid as soon as he could get her unclothed and into his bed once she was healed.

"Is something the matter, Will?" Doubt laced her tone, and he snapped out of his daze.

"The only thing that is wrong, is that ye arenae yet my wife, and we must correct that now. Ye look beautiful, Mary."

"Aye, ye do." Looking his sister up and down, James seemed to glow with pride. "Now, hold yer son, Mary, so I may help William walk ye there," he said gruffly, and William enjoyed watching James squirm every time he attempted to be sentimental.

"I have a better idea." William swooped her off her feet. Mary squealed and wrapped her arms around his shoulders. "'Tis a long walk and I want ye to be able to stand for the ceremony."

"Och, ye arenae wedded just yet. Ye cannae carry the bride!" James protested halfheartedly from behind, but William ignored him.

Giving her a soft, sweet kiss, William began to walk down the long corridor with his bride in his arms. She was so light, so frail, and he hoped she was strong enough for a quick ceremony. "Are ye certain ye want this, Mary? 'Tis not too late. We can wait until ye have more strength."

"Nay, Will. I am ready. I can do this." Mary kissed his forehead, and they continued toward the cathedral where kin from three clans awaited them as James walked behind with their new son.

As the crowd quieted and parted for William, he saw Father Benjamin standing in front of the altar, a smile on his wrinkled cheeks, clearly happy to be performing their marriage. When William set Mary on her feet and supported her weight, James handed wee William to her and stood on her other side as the women in the crowd pointed and cooed when they saw wee William's face.

"I am pleased to see that Mary has so many who love her and have come all this way to prove it," the priest said in his shaky voice. "We see so many come through those doors and their stories seldom have a happy ending. I am grateful to give ye yers, my lady. Few people are as spirited and strong as ye."

"My thanks, Father," Mary smiled, holding her bairn and looking up at William with a gleam in her eyes that let him know just how happy she truly was.

The priest began the ceremony in the traditional Latin language, reciting a few liturgies before jumping into the Gaelic vows, knowing Mary was not strong enough to stand for overlong.

"Blood of my blood and bone of my bone. I give ye my body, that we two might be one. I give ye my spirit, 'til our life shall be done." They repeated these vows in tandem, and William stared into her bright hazel eyes and watched as a small tear dripped out of the corner of one side, running down her cheek. Gently wiping it away, William smiled. "I love ye," he silently mouthed, and she did the same, turning pink in the cheeks, yet smiling sheepishly. Never in his life had he expected to love a woman with his entire being, so purely, so earnestly, so suddenly. A sennight ago, William was in misery as he evaded Marjorie, knowing he needed a wife, yet having no desire to wed for convenience. Now, he wed for love of the bonniest lass in Scotland.

A candle behind Mary flickered, and the flutter of a moth circling its flame caught his eyes. Momentarily allowing his gaze to land on the wee insect, how it desired the light and heat, drawn to its mesmerizing flare, unaware that succumbing to the fire's song would set him ablaze, William suddenly understood why a moth would dare to dance with fire. Mary was his flame, and he the moth, caught in her embrace, willing to risk all simply to be warmed by her glow. She emanated comfort when she was calm, raged like an inferno when she was angry, and William would gladly stand outside her fire, grateful to simply be touched by its warmth for all his life.

"Will?" Mary whispered his name and he snapped his gaze back to her, the fire that had lit his entire life aflame. "Rings? Have we any rings?"

Stepping forward, Robert handed the priest two rings and smiled at them both. "They are mine and Lizzie's. Ye will need yer own in due time, but every union to wear those rings for the past two centuries has a been a long, blessed, and happy one." Taking wee William from Mary's arms and stepping back into the crowd, William watched as Robert gently handed the bairn to Elizabeth and reverently touched her abdomen like another hopeless moth caught in the eternal flame of a woman. The two plain bands of silver were blessed by the priest, then he handed one to him, and one to Mary. Once more vows were exchanged, James pulled out his dagger and tore off a piece of each of their plaids, watching as they tied them together in a knot, symbolically uniting the two clans.

Father Benjamin announced them officially married, and the crowd cheered as William gently took Mary in his arms and looked down at her glowing face. "Dinnae look now, Mary, but I do believe there is mistletoe above us." Looking up, Mary saw Robert holding a fresh sprig over her head and she tilted her head back to laugh.

"I suppose that means we must kiss, Sir William Keith, for I hear 'tis bad fortune not to." Mary fluttered her lashes and flashed him a wry smile.

"Well, we cannae allow that, now can we, Lady Mary Keith?"

Gently pulling her into his embrace, William kissed her softly at first, deepening it slightly before pulling away. He had the rest of his life to ravish his wife. They were bound together forever. But for now, she needed rest. Though she smiled and looked around at the crowd, he could see the tiredness in her eyes. She had given birth less than a day ago and, strong woman that she was, it was William's job to make certain she was well cared for.

Scooping her up in his arms, the crowd cheered once more, and William turned to James. "Am I allowed to carry her now, Brother?"

"Aye, ye are her husband now, and I trust ye with her life." Those words, spoken so matter-of-factly, meant the world to William as he walked through the cathedral, holding his wee wife in his arms while their clans surrounded them with celebratory shouts and well wishes.

Arriving at her chamber, William carried his new wife over the threshold and gently placed her on the bed. "There ye are, safe from the spirits that haunt the threshold, my love," he jested and sat down beside her.

Mary went white for the briefest of moments and looked over his shoulder at the corner of the room. Turning his own head, he saw naught but an unlit candle in a brass holder and a table with a basin. "Are ye all right, Mary?"

"Aye. Just… looking for something I once lost," she said cryptically, taking his hand in hers with a smile. "But I have all I need, as long as I have ye and wee William."

Elizabeth walked through the door carrying the bairn and gently handed him over to Mary. "I am so pleased, Mary. We are sisters now! Ye have made my arse of a brother verra happy."

"Hey, what did I do to deserve that?" he asked, scowling at his sister.

"Do ye remember when ye were a wee lad, and ye would always spit on yer finger and shove it into my ear? 'Twas disgusting. Ye ken ye are an arse, Will." Winking at Mary, Elizabeth crossed the room and left, gently shutting the door behind her.

"I dinnae remember such a thing… but I will do my best to make certain wee William never torments his wee sisters," William said with a mischievous grin and stood from the bed, looking at Mary. "How are ye feeling, my love?"

"Like the most fortunate woman in all of Scotland, nay, the world." Gripping her hand, he saw her eyes fluttering closed and knew she had used up all her energy.

"Then I must be the most fortunate man," he replied. "Ye are tired, Mary, and the bairn must eat. Shall I help ye remove yer mother's dress so ye can be comfortable?" Mary nodded and he did as requested, unlacing the bodice and slowly working it down her shoulders and over her hips, pulling it down her legs until she was only in her under tunic. She was the most beautiful woman, and she was his. One day soon, he would make sweet love to her again, but for now, he simply climbed into the bed beside her and their son, watching as she fed the bairn, mesmerized by the sheer beauty of her body as it nurtured wee William.

"I love ye, Mary. My entire world rests in this bed, and when ye are well enough to travel, we will leave for Dunnottar, where ye will be my lady and we will raise many bairns, making love as the waves of the ocean crash against our cliffs. We shall be happy there together, forever." Kissing her lips one last time, William nuzzled into her side and closed his eyes, wondering how a fool like him had won the love of such a woman, and grateful for once that his sister was more stubborn than he. But, he would never admit that she was always right.

CONTENTMENT FLOWED THROUGH her like the calm rocking of the sea, cradling her in its soothing embrace. William's soft breath grazed her arms while he slept, and she watched the rise and fall of his strong chest. Wee William finished nursing and fell fast asleep in her arms.

Mary had been broken. Just a sennight ago, she believed she would never love again, never know happiness with another man. So much had happened in such a short time, and when she recounted the days since the beginning of the Yule and all that had transpired, she realized an entire lifetime could unfold in just a matter of days when one least expected it. She had agreed to marry William for protection, but never had she expected to grow so profoundly in love with him. Though she would miss her kin at Drum, Mary looked forward to a new beginning at Dunnottar, being able to put her skills to use and help the Keith Clan. She knew she would visit Drum often, but not being haunted by Alexander's memory around every corner would be a welcome change.

When she thought of the man she had lost on Harlaw Field that day, a sadness still tugged at her stomach. He'd had so much life to live. But, she found that the harsh, stinging slash of pain that had once felt like a mortal wound, now felt like a tender bruise, only painful when touched. And yet, she could smile now, knowing he was living on in their son and was never truly lost. She had found love again, had found life.

Looking at the unlit candle in the corner of the room, Mary sighed and wondered if she had truly seen Alexander while birthing William, or if it was a mere consequence of her addled brain. "Look what we created, Alex," she whispered with a smile. "Thank ye for loving me and giving me the greatest gift a man can give a woman. Rest easy kenning William will love him as well as we do."

Yawning, Mary snuggled her sleeping bairn against her chest and nuzzled closer to William, feeling her eyes growing heavy as the desperate need for sleep pulled her away.

A second before her eyes closed, she swore she saw the candle flicker to life in the corner, but when she blinked and focused her gaze, the flame was out, nothing but a wisp of smoke drifting from its wick.

Alexander was finally at peace, and so was she.

Author Note

Hello, lovely reader! Thank you so much for reading "Like a Laird to a Flame"! There is so much history wound into the fabric of this book, so I want to take a moment to go through some fun facts about my characters. The best part of being a historical author is doing all the research on people who lived hundreds of years ago, taking the knowledge you can find, and filling in the blanks to create a story that brings them back to life. I strive to keep them relatable. They are flawed. They have goals, fears, less desirable traits, and hurdles to climb, but they come out the other side better people. Isn't that always our goal, as well?

First, let us discuss Sir William Keith who was Laird of Dunnottar Castle, a knight, and Marischal of Scotland, which was a title passed down to the Laird of Dunnottar since the days of the Bruce. The Marischal's responsibility was to protect the king during meetings of Parliament. In the winter of 1411 when this book takes place, King James I of Scotland was still imprisoned by the English, so he would have been protector of the regent, who was King James's uncle, Robert Stewart, who was known as a villain and likely the cause of the king's elder brother's death, a powerplay for the throne.

William was Elizabeth Keith's elder brother, so he was closely tied to the Irvines through the marriage of Elizabeth to Alexander Irvine before he died in Harlaw in July of 1411. She then was made to marry Robert, which is all explained in book one, "For Love of a Laird". William married a woman named Mary Hamilton, who in reality likely never knew the Irvines before her marriage to him, much less had a child with Alexander, though she and William did have a son also named William, and one named Alexander. So, I sort of combined the two.

Mary Hamilton was born in Cadzow, and her brother was James Hamilton, 5th Laird of Cadzow. Their mother was a Hamilton, and their father remains unknown. Perhaps he was an Irvine? In the story, I switched it and had her father as a Hamilton and her mother an Irvine, so she would end up back on Irvine lands when her father passed, crossing paths with Alexander and befriending Elizabeth, who would introduce her to William. It was all my master plan! Muahahaha! Together, Mary and William had four braw laddies!

Let's discuss this interesting character that I introduced to the story: Archibald Douglas, 4th Earl of Douglas. He was from a line of Douglases known as the "Black Douglases" for having been involved in many dark deeds through the generations. In fact, Archibald Douglas likely played a role in helping to capture King James in the early 15th century, which is even darker when you consider that he was married to the king's younger sister, Margaret. So, why would the Irvines consider an alliance with this man? Well, the Douglases were obviously a very well-connected family and owned much land spread across Scotland. They made a formidable foe, but they would make a mighty ally.

I have no idea if the Douglases were ally or foe to the Irvines, though they are not listed as an enemy clan. But, he really did have a daughter named Marjorie who was the youngest of five children. I imagine by the time it came time to marry her off, he simply wished to be done with it. He wasn't very kind to her in the story, was he? Hopefully, the real Archibald at least treated his daughter with more respect. There is no record of who Marjorie married, but a good match would be expected. She was of royal stock, after all, and her attitude proves that she knew as much. But, I plan to help Marjorie grow and mature under Elizabeth's tutelage and, hopefully, we will get to see her make a good match eventually.

Whether Reginald Irvine was their brother is debatable. Almost all records only show two sons belonging to Robert Irvine, 2nd Laird of Drum: Alexander and Robert. However, in my very thorough research, I did find mention of a Reginald Irvine in old documents, so he did exist in some way, whether a brother or a cousin. I felt I needed to include him in my stories. As a third brother, he is certainly more lighthearted and carefree, as the weight of the lairdship does not fall on his shoulders. But, he is loyal and fierce at the same time. I enjoy his character very much and have BIG plans for him in book three. If you want a clue, the title is called "Maid for the Knight". I wonder which maid it could be? I shall let you think about that until it comes out in a few months!

In my attempt to make certain the castle was described accurately, I purchased the excavation notes on the Laird's Hall at Drum Castle, as well as spoke with the kind folks over at Drum who sent me more information. It was a wonderful document that described the cellars very well, what sort of bones and debris were found, and during what months they would be eaten. I looked at maps, blueprints, and models of the tower and surrounding land to create the most realistic recreation for my readers. I hope you feel as if you truly were at Drum Castle while reading this story.

The Yule lasted twelve days, starting the day of the winter solstice. Nobody was allowed to work, so making merry and wassailing were encouraged. The castle would have had evergreens and mistletoe all over, so I wanted those to be included in the scheme to bring Mary and William together. Mistletoe was considered good for fertility and it had already been a tradition to kiss beneath it for centuries. It would have been a time of peace, so it was unfortunate for my characters to have their Yule interrupted by the schemes of the dastardly Stephan and Archibald, but what better time to infiltrate Drum and cause chaos while everyone least expected it?

On a more somber note, Alexander Irvine was placed to rest in the Kirk of St. Nicholas in Aberdeen, just ten miles northeast of Drum

Castle. I imagine it would have taken less than an hour on a horse to arrive there from the castle, depending on weather conditions. I felt it was important for Mary to be forced to face her demons and make peace with the loss of Alexander. That is what inspired me to make certain she ended up there when having her child.

Within that kirk, there is a section in the transept called the Drum Aisle where several Irvine lairds and nobles have been placed to rest, some with effigies. Alexander is one of them, interred after the Battle of Harlaw. To this day, you can visit the kirk and see his effigy, along with Robert, who was called Alexander once he became laird, and Elizabeth's. Though Alexander only played a short role in the first book before his death, he had a huge impact on the arc of this series, so I wanted to make certain he was properly included and honored as an important character, even in death. Here is a sketch of his effigy in the Kirk of St. Nicholas.

I sure hope you enjoyed both my story and this bit of information about the real people who inspired it! I have had so much fun writing and researching for these books, as I am a proud member of the Clan Irvine of Drum and was inspired to write these stories while I was researching my genealogy. Although they were the first people to strike my fancy and inspire a story, I later discovered I am a direct descendant of Robert and Elizabeth, who are my 14th great-grandparents. So, these stories truly are a piece of my heart, and I thank you for taking the time to read them!

Sincerely,
Mia

About the Author

Mia is a full-time mother of two rowdy boys, residing in the SF Bay Area. As a child, she often wrote stories about fantastic places or magical things, always preferring to live in a world where the line between reality and fantasy didn't exist.

In High school, she entered writing contests and had some stories published in small newspapers or school magazines. As life continued, so did her love of writing. So one day, she decided to end her cake decorating business, pull out her laptop and fulfill her dream of writing and publishing novels. And she did.

When Mia isn't writing books or chasing her sweaty children around a park, she loves to drink coffee by the gallon, get lost in a good book, hike with her family and drink really big margaritas with her friends! Her happy place is the Renaissance Faire, where you can find her at the joust, rooting for the shirtless highlander in a kilt.

Website: www.miapride.com
FB: facebook.com/miaprideauthor
Amazon: amazon.com/Mia-Pride/e/B01M6VEWGX
Instagram: instagram.com/mia_pride_author
Twitter: twitter.com/mia_pride
BookBub: https://www.bookbub.com/profile/mia-pride